TOMB RAIDING PHD

TOMB RAIDING PHD

I FEAR NO EVIL BOOK FIVE

MARTHA CARR
MICHAEL ANDERLE

LMBPN

DISRUPTIVE IMAGINATION

TOMB RAIDING PHD TEAM

Thanks to the JIT Readers

Angel LaVey
James Caplan
John Ashmore
Peter Manis
Daniel Weigert
Larry Omas
Mary Morris
Keith Verret

If we've missed anyone, please let us know!

DEDICATIONS

From Martha

To everyone who still believes in magic
and all the possibilities that holds.
To all the readers who make this
entire ride so much fun.
And to my son, Louie and so many wonderful friends who
remind me all the time of what
really matters and how wonderful
life can be in any given moment.

From Michael

To Family, Friends and
Those Who Love
To Read.
May We All Enjoy Grace
To Live The Life We Are
Called.

Shay crept through the hallway of the darkened Connecticut mansion with Lily trailing close behind. The tomb raider had made a promise to Peyton, and it was time to keep it.

Would have been nice to have his backup for this little job, but he's already freaking out about his brother's hackers, and the last thing I need is him freaking out in my ear as I confront his brother.

Randy Coolidge should have left well enough alone, but the man had let empire-sized greed push him into searching for anything that suggested Peyton might still be alive. If Randy found Peyton he'd find Shay, and then *more* people would have to die.

The idea of killing Randy, a man who'd placed a hit on his own brother, didn't bother her much, but she knew it might destroy Peyton. Time to come up with a different plan.

I'm trying to keep you alive, Randy. You better fucking play along.

Lily all but glided behind the tomb raider. The teen Gray Elf's footsteps barely caused a creak from the hardwood floors as the pair closed on their target's room.

Shay gave the girl a nod. Lily nodded back. Her ski mask gave the whole situation a sinister air. The home invasion had been surprisingly easy. Randy had a lot of money, but not a lot of security. Usually, the kind of man who would casually order another man's death was a little more paranoid. The lack of security suggested he thought he had no reason to be afraid.

The arrogant ass probably thought he didn't need it for his remote home. Shay would enjoy puncturing his ego. That night he'd learn why he was never safe.

"Ready?" whispered Shay.

Lily nodded.

Time to get scared, Randy. Time to get as scared as Peyton, you asshole.

Shay kicked open the door and whipped out her 9mm. Lily flipped on the light switch near the door, but Randy Coolidge didn't jerk awake or pull out a hidden weapon or artifact. Instead, the deadly threat to Peyton, the vicious brother who put out a hit on his own family member, continued snoring in his mammoth bed, oblivious to the ski-masked intruders standing in front of him.

"You've got to be fucking kidding me," Shay mumbled. A dramatic entrance was pointless without an audience.

Lily chuckled. "It just means we did a good job sneaking in here. We're just too good."

"Part of Operation Christmas Carol depends on making an impression on the man." Shay gestured at him with her gun. "But the asshole has the gall to be fucking snoring."

Lily frowned. "I'm still not sure I like the name. It's almost summer. It just seems weird, you know?"

"Call it Operation Solstice Carol then. Whatever. I don't give a shit. The point is we need to mindfuck him. Just blowing him away would create more attention and problems, even if the fucker really deserves it." Shay shrugged and pulled out a small copper ring. She tossed it to Lily, and the teen snatched it out of the air. "The gnome yakked for a long time about his standard crap of using this thing for evil and the consequences, so think good thoughts or whatever."

Lily glanced toward Randy. "Does what we're doing count as evil?"

Shay shrugged. "Sometimes there is a very fine line. I'm trying to cut down on the number of people I might have to shoot. Whoever's keeping track has to give us points for that."

Lily eyed the ring. "And you're sure it's safe?"

"It's just going to help us make our thoughts visible. I'd love to have it all the time, but Tubal-Cain looked like he was going to go full Rumpelstiltskin on me and demand my firstborn if I asked for them for more than a couple days. That gnome is useful, but I don't trust him."

Lily snickered and slipped it on, and Shay slipped on a second ring. It was warm to the touch.

The tomb raider marched over to the bed and stared down at Randy. "Wake up, asshole."

He muttered something in his sleep and rolled to his other side.

"I said, wake up, asshole," Shay repeated, this time louder.

Randy's eyes fluttered open, and he stared up at the masked Shay. After a few seconds, he blinked, and his eyes widened.

"Shit."

Shay patted her thigh with her gun. "Just to get this out of the way... Even though I really want to, I don't plan on killing you. If I did, you'd already be dead. You would have never woken up."

Randy's gaze cut between Shay and Lily. "Then why bring the gun?"

"Because it'll keep your attention on me and help persuade you not to do anything stupid that might increase the chance that I actually have to kill you."

"Stupid like what?" Randy frowned but kept his gaze locked on Shay's masked face.

Shay had to admire the man's calm demeanor under pressure.

"Call the cops or security or anything like that. Standard stupid shit."

Randy nodded. "You've got my attention. So, you're here to rob me? You want safe codes or something like that?"

Shay snorted. "Please. I make a lot of money, asshole, and I doubt you even have anything worth stealing. I don't need your crappy paintings or second-rate vases. I'm sure half of them are fakes anyway."

The man's face twisted in indignation. Shay almost

laughed, and Lily didn't hold back her snort. Peyton's brother was more irritated that she'd challenged his wealth than that she stood at his bedside with a gun. Such great priorities.

Randy crossed his arms over his chest. "If you're not here to kill me, and you're not here to rob me, why *are* you here?"

"To give you a glimpse into the past, present, and future. To let you understand that your present path will lead to ruin. And maybe, just maybe, you'll heed my warning and change your life before it's too late."

Randy frowned, again looking between the intruders. "What the hell are you talking about?"

Tension suffused Shay's muscles. Not being able to take care of the problem with brute force or skillful hacking made everything difficult. It was time for a little old-fashioned psychological manipulation. She needed Randy to accept that what he was doing would be a disaster, but she also needed to provide a reason to believe that her proposed solution would work. That required a little priming.

Even the rings, which would project images from their minds, wouldn't help if Randy didn't think Lily could see the future.

Of course, she *could*. The problem was she could only see fifteen minutes into the future. Not that their mark needed to know that.

Time to see how useful you are, Tubal-Cain.

Shay mentally envisioned the activation glyph for the ring.

A ghostly image of Peyton winked into existence just

above Randy's bed. The ghost Peyton lay in a pool of his own blood, and crimson covered his face from the bullet wound in his forehead.

Randy scurried backward, hissing.

Damn, that looks realistic. I did a good job of faking his death the first time. Maybe I missed my calling as a special-effects make-up artist.

"That's nasty," Lily murmured.

"Don't worry." Shay chuckled. "You know how this goes, right, Randy?"

"My name is Randall."

"Sure, whatever, Randy. The point is, don't worry. You can see the Ghosts of Christmas Past, Present, and Future, but you can't touch them."

Randy snorted. "You're supposed to be the Ghost of Christmas Past? Please."

Shay shook her head. "Nah. We're more like Jacob Marley." She pointed toward the image of Peyton. "That's the ghost."

"What's the point of this?" Randy spat.

"I already explained. It's about making you see the error of your ways, so we need to start with the past, Randy. Can't understand the future without understanding the past and the present, right?"

"What's the point of showing me my dead brother?" His voice quivered at the word dead.

Yeah, thanks for confirming it.

Shay leaned forward and snorted. "There's something there you don't believe."

Randy gritted his teeth and looked away. "Screw you."

"Sorry, not my type, asshole."

His hands clenched into fists. "That's what you are? Some thugs my brother hired in revenge?" He snorted. "I'm surprised he finally gathered his balls."

"That's strange. I thought you just said your brother was dead."

"*Bullshit* he's dead. I know his death was faked." Randy sneered. "You know what? I'm not begging you." He pointed at Lily. "Or you."

"Aw, but begging's fun to hear," Lily goaded.

"Screw you both. I've done nothing wrong. I've only protected my interests and my rights."

Shay barked out a laugh. "Seriously? I think hiring a man to kill your brother ranks pretty high up there on the Naughty List. You've got a seriously skewed perspective on life there, Randy."

"Why come here and do any of this? All you've done is confirm Peyton's alive. If this was some brilliant plan to convince me otherwise, it's failed horribly."

"No. Peyton Coolidge is dead." Shay pointed to the image. "He died that day. Problem is a certain someone won't stop coming after him, so we've come to show you, Randy Scrooge, where you're gonna end up if you keep chasing a ghost."

A quick mental conjuring of another symbol wiped out Peyton's image.

Shit. I would have just preferred some sort of incantation than having to concentrate like that. No wonder most magic doesn't use that kind of thing.

Randy shuddered.

Little more freaked out than we're letting on, huh? Good. I can work with that.

"What's next?" he asked. "Going to show me his rotting corpse in the ground?"

"Nope. Consider me the Ghost of Christmas Present."

"I thought you were supposed to be Jacob Marley."

"I've got theatrical range." Shay shook her head. "As for showing you a corpse, nope. Kind of pointless, don't you think? I'm more interested in showing you your future. After all, you're the one who isn't dead."

"My brother isn't either."

"He's dead enough." Shay pointed to Lily. "And the Ghost of Christmas Future over there is going to show you where you'll end up if you keep looking for him."

Randy snorted. "The future? Please. Your friend there can't see the future."

Lily took a deep breath. A spectral image of Randy appeared near the wall. He sat, leaning against a brick wall. He had a shaggy and an unkempt beard. His clothes were in tatters, and a hand-painted sign was lying on the ground next to him.

HUNGRY AND HOPELESS. PLEASE GIVE. GOD BLESS.

Shay resisted a face-palm. She should have been a little more specific about what image to sell to the man. Whatever happened to Randy Coolidge in the far future, the tomb raider doubted it'd involve him begging on a street corner.

Prison would be nice, but she'd settle for him just leaving Peyton the hell alone.

The incredulous look on Randy's face suggested he didn't buy the pathetic vision of the future either.

Time to sell this shit.

"That's what waits for you if you keep going after the ghost of your brother, Randy," Shay insisted.

"Bullshit."

Shay had to give the man credit. Most men would have been more intimidated by the presence of two ski-masked intruders, especially one with a gun. Randy had a definite hard edge his brother lacked.

The man rolled out of bed and marched over to his homeless specter. "This is what you expect me to believe? This is nothing but illusions. Tricks. You think you can impress me with something any half-rate witch could pull off?"

Lily frowned. "Not illusions. The future, you arrogant ass."

Shay nodded her agreement.

"The future? You expect me to believe you can see the future? You sound like a kid. What, you show up with some twelve-year-old boy and expect me to be scared?"

Lily snorted. She was more insulted at the idea Randy thought she was a tween boy than his disbelief in her abilities.

Shay sighed. *Maybe I need to sell the danger a teensy bit more to this asshole.*

She marched right up to Randy and slammed a fist into his stomach. He howled and dropped to the ground clutching his middle.

Sometimes a little pain can be clarifying, and this asshole needs to get that we mean business.

"If you're going to kill me," he wheezed, "then just go ahead and do it. Like I told you before, I won't beg. I never beg."

Shay rolled her eyes. "And I told you already this isn't about killing you, but if you don't believe me about the future, why don't you give my friend here a little test? Something that we can see in the next few minutes. That way nobody has to wait around in the middle of the night."

Pain still lining his face, Randy managed to sit up. "You can see the future?" He nodded toward a clock on the wall. "In one minute, I'll stick fingers up behind my back. How many? And thirty seconds after that, how many will I change to?"

Lily scoffed. "That's easy. It'll be—"

"Write it down," Shay commanded. "That way he can't try and play games."

The Gray Elf's ability to see the future had a lot of implications concerning the nature of cause and effect that Shay didn't even want to think about. She needed to at least minimize the chance of Randy screwing up the use of an already unreliable power.

Shay walked over to a desk in the corner of the room and grabbed an expensive monogrammed fountain pen and a notepad. She handed them to Lily and enjoyed Randy's glare.

The girl scribbled down two numbers with a frown. She gave the pad back to Shay, and the tomb raider turned it away from Randy.

Only the steady tick of the clock kept the silence at bay as everyone waited. The first minute passed, and Randy held up his fingers. Two.

Shay didn't react. The next half-minute ticked by, and the man held up five fingers.

Fuck. If I don't show him, he'll know something's up.

Shay turned the pad around. Two and four.

Randy narrowed his eyes. "What the fuck does that mean?"

"She got the first one. She can see the future, asshole."

"But she didn't get both, and I'm supposed to believe she can see far in the future? Give me a break."

Shay handed the pen and pad to Lily. She walked over to Randy and pulled up the bottom of her mask, so he could better appreciate her vicious smile. "Short-term visions are harder than long-term visions," she offered. She had no idea if that was true, so it wasn't technically a lie. "But I can tell you something. The future has a way of coming true when people try to help it along." She lifted her gun. "If you don't stop chasing this ghost, by the time I'm done your suffering will be the thing of legend. And after I've had all my fun..." she pointed the gun at his crotch, and his eyes widened, "I'm *still* not gonna kill you. I'm gonna leave you broke and alone to rot away in the underbelly of society among all the people you were too smug to even look at before. Your money will be gone. Your influence will be gone. You'll be nothing but a pile of flesh and bones waiting to die."

The defiant fire faded from Randy's eyes, and he swallowed. "What if I don't believe you?"

"Pick another number."

Shay nodded at Lily. Her hands were behind her back, her fist clenched around the pen and pad.

We both knew your powers can be annoying. Don't worry, just pull it off. We've almost got him.

Randy nodded quickly. "Okay, one minute."

Lily half-closed her eyes, took a deep breath, and then scribbled down another number.

Don't make me kill you, Randy. I don't want to have to kill you, if only because it'll bring more attention to Peyton. But you're going out of your way to force me.

Randy held up three fingers.

Lily turned the pad. Three.

The man frowned and stared at the pad for a long moment. Grim determination ate at the disbelief covering his face. "But the authorities don't believe he's dead."

Shay shrugged. "They'll give up soon enough. Now, the question is, will you?" She lifted the 9mm but didn't point it at the man.

Randy nodded slowly. "Yes."

"Good. Glad you can be reasonable. You going to stop poking around in the past?"

"Yeah. Yeah, I can do that."

Shay smiled. "Then you'll have a happy summer."

They'd driven for about ten minutes before Lily spoke.

"I'm sorry." She brushed a few strands of gray hair out of her eyes. "It's not going to work, is it? He doesn't believe anything because of the screwed-up divination."

Shay shrugged. "Not sure, but I think two out of three isn't bad. The combination of the implied threat with the possibility of ending up on the street will be enough to keep him quiet."

"But what if it isn't?"

"We'll worry about that if it happens."

I'll show him a different future. One that ends a lot more abruptly and painfully.

Shay shot the worried-looking teen a smile. Ending this the old way might be her only choice, but Lily didn't need to be involved in it. Maybe it was silly to worry about the girl's innocence, but Shay knew all too well what a few teenage murders could do to a person.

"Well, we're on the East Coast," Shay commented. "Anything you want to see before we head back to LA? I need to get the rings back to the gnome by tomorrow night, but otherwise no time pressure."

"It's only a couple of hours to New York, right?"

"Yeah, what about it?"

"I want to see Central Park." An eager gleam appeared in the elf's gray eyes.

Shay sighed. "It's not *that* cool. It's just a big park."

"Have you seen satellite photos of New York? It's damned cool. Central Park is just this nice little rectangle of green in the middle of a massive maze of gray."

"Fine. Central Park it is. But we're gonna do it my way."

Lila glanced at Shay. "Your way?"

Shay grinned. "Yeah, you'll see."

2

D angerous. That was what wandering New York was for a woman like Shay.

I shouldn't be hanging out in New York. I took out the Nuevo Gulf Cartel, but that doesn't mean I'm safe. It's not like I haven't pissed off other people around here, even after *I died.*

Shay and Lily jogged their way across the stone Gapstow Bridge. The moonlight and the light from the surrounding buildings reflected off the water below. The relative quiet of the night along with the reflected light gave the whole walk a tranquil quality despite the tension lingering in Shay's stomach.

"Your way is making me exercise?" Lily asked.

"Yep. That way I can justify this as training rather than just some pointless tourist crap."

"I haven't seen as much of the world as you."

Shay grinned. "Train as a tomb raider and you will. First, though, you need to toughen up."

A simple walk around Central Park might have been a

waste of time, but a run would at least provide some exercise for the day. The junior tomb raider had come a long way, but she still lacked Shay's sheer physicality. Her ridiculous reflexes wouldn't help her if she collapsed from exhaustion. Sometimes the best way to win was simply to outlast your enemy.

"But since we're here, it might be nice to see some of the tourist stuff." Shay smiled at Lily. "It's too bad it's so late. We can't visit the zoo."

"They have a zoo in this park? That's what I'm talking about. That's how big it is."

Shay shrugged. "I guess."

They ran by a sleeping homeless man curled up on a bench. It was the sixth homeless person they'd passed in as many minutes.

Lily frowned when Shay glanced her way.

"Problem?" Shay asked.

The teen shook her head. "I'm fine."

"You don't look fine. What? Does seeing homeless here bother you because *you're* homeless? Not everywhere has abandoned nuclear escape tunnels to live in."

"I'm not homeless."

Lily sped up.

Shay matched her speed. "You're not?"

Lily shook her head. "Even when I'm not staying with you, I have a place to stay. I have a home and friends. That's the difference."

"Whatever works. It's *your* life. I'm gonna teach you how to be a tomb raider, but you have to figure the rest of it out yourself."

Conversation faded, and only the sound of their

running shoes striking the rock, dirt, and asphalt cut through the night.

Lily hissed a few minutes later and shook her head. "We need to hurry. Now."

"What's wrong?"

"I had a vision. There's some assholes. Big guys, maybe Mafia. They are going to kill a homeless man. They're going to laugh about it and talk about how they think they're doing good stuff." Lily's jaw clenched. "We don't have much time." Her pace quickened again.

The pair continued running along the asphalt path, sweat beading their foreheads. Lily's gift might not always be reliable, but such a specific vision wasn't in question.

Even with the influence of Alison and James, Shay was not interested in being a do-gooder, but that didn't mean she was okay with random fuckers murdering some poor man for kicks. Not to mention, there was no way in hell Lily would ever trust her again if she tried to walk away.

There was no strong reason not to get involved. It wasn't like Yulia was at the other end of the park waiting for her. A little nighttime workout might be fun. It'd also be a good opportunity to test Lily's hand-to-hand training in a relatively controlled setting that wouldn't involve witches or competing heavily-armed tomb raiders.

The density of homeless dropped. A few even hurried in the opposite direction.

We must be getting close.

Lily continued running ahead, taking long strides. Her face was set in grim determination.

Worried it could have as easily been one of your friends back home?

They arrived at the sprawling Terrace. The glow of the path's lights illuminated the mustard-colored sandstone covering the entire area. In the center of the Terrace was a multi-tier fountain nestled in a plant-festooned stone-lined pond.

A cowering old man in a worn jacket, jeans, and boots knelt in front of the fountain. His face was covered with blood, and he held his arms over his head. Eight men in dark suits with slick-backed hair surrounded him.

One of the men delivered a vicious kick to the man's stomach, and the victim cried out.

Oh shit. Well, I guess if we do this quick enough, it's not like they'll even have a chance to report me to someone who might recognize me. Plus, this is straight-up bullshit.

"Come on, guys," Shay called. "Seriously? Beating up an old homeless man?"

One of them looked her way and snorted. "This ain't your business, bitch."

Killing the men was low on the list of good ideas for multiple reasons, but it would be tricky to take them down without killing or seriously maiming them given their numbers. Unlike James, she couldn't punch a man through a wall.

Maybe she could still get them to leave without a fight.

Shay shrugged. "I'm just saying eight badasses like you can do better. Find someone worth your time."

"You don't get it. Scum like him infest our streets, our parks, and nobody does anything about it. Well, I talked to my boys, and we all agreed that if we do a little cleaning, most of these roaches will go scurrying along."

Lily ground her teeth and stepped forward, but stopped when Shay raised a hand.

I know you're mad, but keep it cool. I can still get them to leave without a fight. I hope.

Shay snorted. Lily probably wanted to rip the men apart on general principles. There was nothing impressive about beating up people who were that much weaker than you, especially when you outnumbered them. The tomb raider only did it when people threatened her life.

She looked the men up and down. Everything about them screamed Mafia. "You Connected?"

The man sneered. "If you're smart enough to know that, then you're smart enough to mind your business. Now get the fuck out of here and let us finish what we started."

Lily trembled with rage. "How could you beat up on some defenseless old man? You asses."

The man kicked the homeless man again. The old man whimpered.

"Fuck this roach. You some bleeding heart, kid?" He narrowed his eyes. "You look freaky. I bet you're Oriceran."

"Screw you, asshole."

The man laughed and pointed at her. "What? You some elf bitch? Look at this elf bitch, boys. You come to New York and smart off to us, bitch? This ain't some tree city shit back on Oriceran. I don't know what sort of whack-ass bullshit you do there, but this is America, and we clean up our messes." He looked at Shay. "Why don't you and your elf bitch run along before you get hurt? My patience is starting to run out."

Shay sighed. So much for convincing the men to leave without trouble, but it was always nice to have a clear

19

conscience before she beat the shit out of someone. She advanced slowly, and his hands twitched.

No knives. No guns. No grenades. I can't leave a trail of bodies in New York, of all places, and certainly not in front of Lily, even if she wouldn't mind so much this time. Didn't expect so many guys, though.

The teen trailed behind her mentor.

"Time to put those reflexes and our sparring training to the test, and I guess it'll be a good tactical exercise being outnumbered," Shay commented. "Let's just knock their asses out and get the hell out of here."

The man snorted. "Get a load of this slut! She thinks she's going to take us out."

"No. I know *we're* gonna take you out."

All the men burst out in loud laughter. With their attention diverted from him, the homeless man started crawling away.

Good instincts. Get the fuck out of here, old man.

One of the other men noticed and frowned at the old man. "He's leaving. We're not done with you, fucker."

Shay sighed and nodded to Lily. The tomb raider and her protégé rushed the mobsters, but the men didn't react. Instead, they all smirked as if being attacked was the most hilarious thing that had happened to them in a while.

The smirks and smiles vanished seconds later. Shay delivered three quick punches in rapid succession. The first man's nose crunched from her attention, and he doubled over after her stomach blow. She'd taken down much larger guys than him during sparring at the gym, let alone during jobs.

Lily might lack her mentor's strength, but she snapped

a solid kick into one of the mobsters' knees. Shay wasn't sure if the snap she heard was her imagination or real, but the man collapsed, screaming.

The six remaining mobsters stepped back, bringing up their fists with deep frowns on their faces. They hadn't expected much resistance.

But they continued to underestimate Shay and Lily, or they would have gone for their guns.

I can work with this. We can finish these assholes off without giving anyone a reason to come sniffing on the other side of the country.

One of the men grunted and threw a punch. Shay ducked the attack and slammed her knee into his crotch, and he howled and fell.

Lily danced around the punches of her opponent. Punch after punch missed by an inch as she bobbed and weaved. Her reflexes served her well. She made a hummingbird look slow.

Two of the men yelled and charged Shay at the same time. She smirked until she saw the man's hand reaching behind him.

Shit. Do I go for my gun?

Shay spun to avoid the first man, but her hesitation allowed the other man to flip his butterfly knife into a ready position.

A third mobster circled her. Apparently, they all sensed she was the greater threat. Lily was still doing a good job of dodging and returned a quick jab or two against the huge thug. He grunted with each hit, but she hadn't managed to land a strike anywhere that might take him down.

Shay stepped back to avoid the swipe of the knife, still

unsure if she should pull out one of her weapons. Two of the men rushed her from the other side. A palm strike to the first one's throat sent him to the ground gasping, and she followed with an elbow toward the other, but the man blocked it with his arm.

His friend used the opening to rush forward, and he slashed at Shay. She hissed as the knife made contact. Blood dripped from her side.

The tomb raider gritted her teeth, resisting the urge to end everything in a hail of gunfire. Her side throbbed.

Fucker.

Lily peppered her opponent with quick strikes. He stumbled, and his movements slowed. She was wearing him down.

Got to finish this shit up.

"Fuck this," one of Shay's attackers yelled, and he went for his gun.

Shay ignored the other two men and leapt, bringing up her knee. The would-be gunman's head snapped back, and he collapsed to the ground. His gun clattered against the sandstone paving.

A hard yank on Shay's arm brought her around. One of the thugs had gotten his hand on her.

His knife friend charged, holding the blade low. Shay slammed her elbow into her captor's face several times until he dropped his arm and grabbed his blood-gushing nose. She leapt to the side, and the knife fighter threw his blade.

Shay hissed in pain as the blade embedded itself in her shoulder.

This is what I get for not just killing all these assholes.

Lily landed a nice solid kick in her enemy's stomach, and he groaned and fell to his knees. The three punches that followed knocked him to the ground.

Shay's two wounds ached. She took a quick step toward the knife guy and throat-punched him before he grabbed his gun. She shoved the falling man into his friend.

They stumbled together, which gave the tomb raider the time she needed to finish her approach. A roundhouse kick knocked out the first man, and a few quick jabs had the other on the ground moaning.

Shay stomped toward the only man in close to fighting shape. He knelt on the ground, blood still gushing from his nose. She slammed a fist into his face to knock him out.

Some of the enemies lay unconscious, and some were awake but groaning. The homeless man they'd been beating before had long since run.

Lily looked at Shay with concern. "You okay?" She shook out her fists, wincing. "Sorry I couldn't help much."

"You did well, especially given your size. A lot of girls your size couldn't take out a normal man, let alone a thug like Goliath over there." Shay sucked in a deep breath. "I didn't want to have to kill anyone, so we did well, all things considered." Her wounds weren't deep, but they weren't scratches either. "I'll live, and we've made our point. Let's get the hell out of here."

They jogged away from the beat-down mobsters. Shay glanced over her shoulder and barely resisted a laugh at a sudden realization.

You lucky assholes. I'm the kinder, gentler Shay. And damn, *you wouldn't have liked what James would have done to you.*

"I think that's enough sightseeing for one day, Lily. Let's

hop in the car so I can get some bandages on. Then let's get the fuck back to Hartford, and fly the hell back to L.A."

Shay eyed the ten-foot diameter pipe that led off into the darkness. LA's underground nuclear escape tunnels were a relic from a time when the local government laughably thought they could provide a path to the mountains for people to evade a nuclear holocaust. The decades had passed and the worries about nuclear annihilation had given way to worries about magic, but no one had ever bothered to seal the tunnels.

The tomb raider had already returned the borrowed magic rings to Tubal-Cain. Now, she just needed to drop off Lily with her friends, even if the idea made her uneasy. She wished Lily would decide she'd rather live in a warehouse than some creepy-ass tunnels, but the girl had insisted on returning to her friends.

What am I even thinking? Lily was doing fine before she ever met me, and the more she's around me, the greater the chance I'm gonna have to explain to James why I've kept her a secret.

But every girl has a few secrets, right? And better than anyone, I can understand not wanting to leave behind friends who actually have your back.

"Every time I'm in here I feel like some killer clown-monster is gonna jump me," Shay grumbled, desperate to focus her mind on something else.

Lily laughed from in front of her. "Who knows? Maybe one will, but I bet you could take him."

"Maybe. I've tangled with a lot of weird shit since

becoming a tomb raider." Shay shrugged. "Good place for your friends to hide. I'm guessing even AET wouldn't want to wander around in here for too long. You could hide a whole *vodyanoy* army down here."

"*Vodyanoy?*"

"Creepy frog guys."

"And you've run into these things?"

Shay nodded. "Yeah. Russia's a fun place. I've made a lot of interesting friends and enemies there."

The deeper they traveled, the darker it got. Shay used her wrist light to cut through the gloom.

Lily led the way through the forks and other junctions as they continued deeper into the tunnel system. The girl hummed quietly to herself, and Shay didn't say much. The tight and unfamiliar environment left her on edge. Even though she'd been in the tunnels before, they weren't home for her like they were for Lily. They were just another dark hole that might be hiding an enemy.

Every second I'm in here makes me tense, but Lily and her friends feel safer here than they do outside. Funny how that works.

After a few minutes, the pair arrived at a triple junction. One of the paths branched off to a much smaller tunnel.

Shay pointed at the smaller tunnel. "What's with that?"

"Oh, that leads to where the escape tunnels meet the old subway tunnels. They connect in several places."

"It's just weird thinking about how many large, strange openings into the darkness exist under cities." Shay snickered.

A distant rumble shook the tunnel.

Shay groaned and braced herself against the nearby wall. "Seriously? An earthquake now?"

Lily shook her head. "Not an earthquake."

The tremor grew in strength, shaking the entire tunnel, and a loud whoosh joined the shaking.

"What the fuck is that?" Shay shouted above the whoosh.

The whoosh changed pitch and grew distant, and the shaking began to subside.

"Express train," Lily explained.

"Express train?" Shay blinked and stared at Lily. "Underground, in abandoned tunnels?"

"Perfect place for the magicals' express train to Europe, don't you think? No one comes poking around and they use spells to keep the shaking from reaching anyone's machines, so no one ever comes looking." Lily shrugged. "Or that's at least what Harry told me."

"Not like the cops or anyone else has come down here, so someone must be doing something right."

Lily held a hand up, and Shay stopped. The tomb raider went for her gun, but Lily shook her head.

"It's nothing dangerous," the teen elf explained. "It's just…we're close to where Harry and the rest are camped for the night. If I come walking in with a stranger, everyone will scatter. By the time we get it all explained, everyone will be freaked out."

"But I've met Harry, and they've seen me."

"Some have. It doesn't matter. We have to be careful. Instincts. I just don't want everyone all spun up." She shrugged.

Shay shook her head. "You don't have to sleep in these

tunnels, Lily. You can come sleep in the warehouse—for a few nights at least."

"I don't need to. I have a place to stay and friends."

"It's hard for me just to turn around and leave you here, and not help you fix things."

Lily shook her head. "You still don't get it. There's nothing that needs fixing." She sighed. "I'll see you soon."

An owl hoot echoed through the tunnels.

They have owls down here?

Lily's eyes widened, and she took off running with a panic-stricken look on her face.

3

S hay blinked. "What the fuck?"

She wasn't sure why an owl had freaked the girl out so much, but there was no way she'd abandon Lily because a few teens might get scared. The tomb raider sprinted after the Gray Elf.

A wereowl? Is there such a thing? I've heard of bird shifters and bird creatures, but I don't know.

The teen didn't look back. She kept running through the tunnels until she hit a junction with four new tunnels.

Shay skidded to a stop, now even more confused. Harry stood panting in the middle of the junction, and sweat dripped down his face.

The boy turned to Lily. "Thank God you heard the distress call. Never know how far it's going to reach."

Footsteps echoed down the tunnels. Shay reached for her gun then dropped her hand as several more teens rushed into the junction. Shay recognized some of them, but not all. She assumed they were all part of Harry's merry little band.

"What's going on?" Lily asked.

Harry sucked in a breath. "A group was out scavenging supplies, but they're in trouble. Some bounty hunters are on their tail. Nasty guys."

"Scavenging?" Shay arched a brow. "Bounty hunters don't come after people for picking cans. You sure you've got that right?"

The teen shrugged. "Look, we take what we need to survive. A lot of people out there have more than they need."

"So you mean you were *stealing.*"

His defiant eyes locked with Shay's. "I'm not apologizing for doing what we need to."

"I'm not asking you to, Harry. I'm just trying to get a feel for what's going on."

I shouldn't get involved. This isn't my business. If I get wrapped up with bounty hunters, it might lead to trouble and cause the wrong people to look my way.

Harry nodded to Lily and the new arrivals. "We need to get going. I know a shortcut we can use to catch up, but we don't have much time."

Shay sighed and rubbed the back of her neck.

Am I really going to let some bounty hunters beat down a bunch of desperate homeless kids? It's not like I can judge them for stealing. I was murdering people for money when I was their age. They're fucking saints compared to me then and now.

"I'll help," Shay announced. "I can deal with a bounty hunter or two." She nodded toward the other teens. "And I'm more than enough to help you out. More people just means more targets for the bounty hunters, and I guarantee I have a lot more experience fighting than any of you."

Lily blinked, then smiled. "Thanks, Shay."

"Fine," Harry shouted. "But we need to go *now.*" He pointed at a wispy blonde girl. "Casey, you come, too. We might need a little witch help."

The girl nodded.

Harry ran off, and the other three fell in behind him. The boy ran like a rocket, not explaining anything as he sprinted from tunnel to tunnel and passed through forks and junctions. The footsteps and heavy breaths of the group echoed, along with the occasional splash as they struck puddles.

They have the run of the city under here. They could do some seriously dangerous shit if they wanted.

Harry's shortcut brought them to a tall ladder that he scurried up. Lily followed, then Casey. Shay brought up the rear.

When Harry reached the top, he hit what appeared to be a sealed manhole cover. He quickly traced a pattern with his finger along the cover, and it glowed, then flew off with a pop.

"Come on! We don't have much time."

The rescue team emerged into a darkened alley within a minute. Harry kicked the manhole cover back onto the hole, and it shimmered and blurred until it looked like the rest of the asphalt in the alley. Perfect camouflage.

How many of these things do they have around town? Do they have one near my place?

They'd arrived in an older business district. The flaking

paint, occasional barred windows, and rusted signs were proof the decades hadn't been kind to the area.

Shay's head shot up at loud shouts from above. Several dark forms leapt from building to building. A moment later, mocking laughter cut through the air, and several more people jumped across.

The tomb raider's eyes narrowed, and her jaw tightened. Even at a distance, she spotted familiar colors. The boy had been wrong, and that changed the entire situation.

"Good news, Harry. They aren't bounty hunters."

Harry stared at her. "You sure? One of the others said he spotted bounty hunters. That's when I broke off to go find help." He frowned. "Who the hell are they, then?"

"That's the bad news. They are Demon Generals."

Lily, Casey, and Harry grimaced at the mention of the vicious street gang.

Good. At least these kids have enough street smarts to be afraid of the gang.

Shay turned to Lily. "Any visions?"

The girl shook her head. "I...can't see anything." She frowned and looked away.

"We'll just deal with what's in front of us, then." Shay searched the alley for some way to get to the roof and spotted a convenient drain pipe. "If a bunch of these guys end up dead, it'll only be worse for you. They'll come looking in force, and it'll also get the cops involved."

The teens nodded.

Shay started shinnying up the pole. "But if we knock 'em around a little and run, that shouldn't be a big deal. Just need to catch up and distract them so your friends can get away."

The tomb raider and the three teens made it to the roof in time to see the gang members leaping after the others.

Fucking Demon Generals. When did they get so brave?

Shay and the others rushed toward the edge and leapt at the same time. They landed with practiced rolls that maintained all their momentum.

The teens in front of the gang members hit a fire-escape and jumped off it to a narrow ledge on the original building. They pushed off the ledge and hopped down to another similar-sized ledge. The gang members took one look at the ledge and rushed down the stairs instead.

Not so brave now, are you, assholes?

Several shouts sounded from the ground. A pack of Demon Generals was closing in from both sides.

Fuck.

Harry, Lily, Shay, and Casey stopped and looked around.

The teens would be able to get away if only the first set of criminals had been a concern, but with three groups of gang members now on them, escape looked a lot less likely.

Shay sighed. "Damn it. I'll handle the guys on the ground. If the others can just shake the guys following them, this'll work." With her heart pounding, she hopped down to a balcony right beneath her. She landed with a thump, then leapt from balcony to balcony until she hit the narrow street.

Fuck. There's no way I can stop both groups without killing a bunch of them. Even if I take the guys on one side out, the others will probably go for their guns. Guess I have no choice.

Shay reached for her gun.

A sudden hard gust of wind howled, shoving back one

of the groups of Demon Generals on the ground. Several of the men hit the ground with loud grunts. Casey stood on the edge of the building with her eyes closed and her hands out in front of her.

I keep forgetting that Lily's not the only special one, even if their shit is unreliable. Just hope Casey can keep it up.

Harry and Lily leapt from the edge of the building, and Shay's heart rate kicked up. It didn't look like they were going to clear the roof. At the last moment, they grabbed the edge of the next roof and pulled themselves up and ran after their friends.

Damn! Impressive.

Shay charged around the corner and approached the four ground-level Demon Generals. They were so focused on tracking their prey and their men above that Shay was able to down two with quick kicks to the knees before they even realized they were under attack.

The two other gang members reached for their guns as they turned around. Shay rushed forward to throat-punch one and slapped the gun out of the second man's hand. With the first man on the ground clutching his throat, she threw a series of quick punches.

All the tattoos in the world didn't make up for a lack of solid training and near-daily practice. The man grunted under her hits, staggering backward. She finished him with an uppercut that sent him to the ground.

Not wanting to repeat her enemies' mistake, Shay didn't turn her back. Instead, she rushed back to the three other men and made sure they were unconscious with a few solid kicks to the head.

She hissed at an ache in her side. The Demon Generals

hadn't hurt her, but she risked opening her wounds from the Central Park fight.

Lily's really dragged me into a lot of unprofitable fights. Don't know how I feel about that, but I might as well finish what I've started. Not like I don't have my own reasons for not liking the Demon Generals.

Shay sprinted in the direction of the fast-moving teens and gangbangers still above her. The howling wind from before had died down, but the reinforcements didn't come around the corner. Maybe Casey's wind had knocked them out.

The front group of teens was closing on a construction site where a massive crane was parked, but there were no decent buildings anywhere nearby. Other than jumping to their deaths, they had no options close enough that Shay could see.

Come on, get the fuck away.

The tomb raider pushed herself, her lungs burning as she tried to catch up. The night might still have to end with gunfire. She wouldn't let assholes like the Demon Generals kill these kids.

The fleeing teens didn't turn. Instead, they dropped straight down off the edge of the building.

"What the fuck?" Shay froze and stared at the teens.

The now-falling teens kicked off the wall, which sent them sailing toward the crane. Shay held her breath as they flew toward the crane and jerked to a halt as they landed on different parts of the boom lattice. Their gloves saved their hands from being shredded, and they immediately scrambled down the boom.

Okay, that was pretty badass. I was getting good at parkour, but I guess I have a lot of things to learn if I want to be on these kids' level. Like always wear gloves.

The Demon Generals who'd chased them stood at the edge of the building. One threw his hands up in the air.

You guys are too chickenshit to try to follow them, or maybe too smart. Just walk away. This shit is over.

Shay looked past the gang members for Harry and Lily. The pair were bounding between the walls of two buildings to make their way back to the ground. She couldn't see Casey.

The Demon Generals milled around on the roof, clearly uncertain what their next move should be.

The teens on the crane reached the ground and disappeared into an alley. Shay sped toward it and caught up with Harry, Lily, and Casey.

"Another hidden manhole cover?" Shay asked between pants.

Harry nodded. "Let's hurry."

"No complaints here."

When they hit the alley, it was empty. Harry ran to the center and knelt, again tracing a pattern with his finger. The manhole cover popped into existence, and he pulled it up. The sweat-covered teen girls hurried in.

Harry gestured to the hole. "Hurry. I've got to seal it."

Shay wasn't used to taking orders from teens, but he was the local expert. She nodded and went to the ladder.

A few minutes later, all the teens and Shay were making their way back toward the main nuclear escape tunnels with Harry in the lead. No one said much of anything as they tried to calm their hearts and catch their breath. A few of the rescued teens eyed Shay with suspicion, but they didn't talk to her.

They reached the original junction where Shay and Lily had run into Harry.

The boy put his fingers to his lips and made another bird call, something more like a songbird than an owl. He sighed and wiped the sweat off his forehead. A few teens popped out of the tunnel with cautious looks on their faces.

Shay glanced at Lily.

"It's his all-clear call," the girl explained.

Harry turned toward the tomb raider, his breathing no longer labored. "Thanks, Shay. First, we saved you, but now you helped save us, and we don't forget things like that." His gaze cut to Lily for a moment, subtle emotion playing on his face.

Not all that long ago Shay might not have recognized that look, but given that she was in a relationship, she could spot love.

Shay took a deep breath and slowly let it out. It'd be best if Lily pulled away from her friends entirely and started a new life, but it wasn't like the tomb raider could ask her to do that. Which meant that if she wanted to help the girl, she'd need to help all of them.

She sighed. Not only that, but she could relate to these kids—even if they all had strange, if unreliable, magic powers. She'd also been forced to make her own way when she was a teenager, and at least Lily and her friends' path didn't involve murder for hire.

Shay offered Harry a slight smile. "If you need anything,

let me know. Supplies, another rescue. Just reach out." She nodded at Lily. "She knows how to get in touch with me."

The tomb raider wasn't worried about the girl betraying the locations of the warehouses. She'd already had the chance and hadn't. Trusting people still tightened Shay's stomach, but between Peyton, James, and Lily, she was slowly getting used to it.

Harry offered his hand. "Same here. I get that you probably don't need supplies from us tunnel rats, but you've seen how we travel all over the city. We see things—things that some people don't want to be seen—so if you ever need good intel or a few extra eyes, we're for hire."

Lily laughed. "Harry's always looking for ways we can make money. Guess that's why he leads us."

Shay shrugged. "Not a bad instinct for a man to have, leader or not."

"Yeah, not bad."

Harry averted his gaze.

Lily sighed. "I need to take you back to the entrance, Shay. I don't think you'll be able to get back yourself."

Shay laughed. "Yeah, without my gadgets, I'm more of a surface kind of woman."

By the time they returned to the entrance, Shay was struck by the extensive knowledge Lily and the other teens had demonstrated about the tunnels under the city. Without that knowledge, they wouldn't have been able to help their friends.

These kids might be more useful than I thought.

Shay sucked in a breath. "You sure you don't want to stay at a warehouse? Way more comfortable than some musty old tunnel."

Lily nodded. "Yeah, I'm sure."

They stared at each for a moment.

Fuck it. I can do warm and fuzzy without kicking someone.

Shay swallowed and leaned in for something very unnatural to her—a friendly hug. "See you around, Lily."

4

An hour later, Shay settled into a chair and sighed. She'd just meant to drop Lily off, not run halfway across the city and fight gangbangers. It'd been a busy couple of nights.

Still, need to get my notes together for my lecture tomorrow. Glad I at least skimmed the material before I went to Connecticut.

As the years passed since her faked death, doubt had crept into her head. One question kept popping up again and again—had she made the right choice, pursuing a career as a tomb raider?

Her original new life plan had been simple enough: make a pile of money, retire, and live the rest of her life on some remote island where no one dangerous would ever think to threaten her. Tomb raiding was a great way to combine her love of history, particularly ancient magical history, with her skills from her old career.

Should I have been playing the stock market instead?

Shay sighed as she flipped open a book, *Huitzilopochtli, Cortez, and the Lost Lake: A New History of Mexico.*

Her life plan had been designed by a woman who trusted no one and had no real friends; by a woman who certainly didn't love anyone. Now, though, she had friends, a boyfriend, and even a protégé. There was even the start of a legitimate career.

The cartel that had forced her into hiding had been destroyed. While she still needed to be careful, the extermination of the Nuevo Gulf Cartel meant she no longer had to constantly look over her shoulder.

Except for all the new enemies I'm making as a tomb raider. Good times.

Shay didn't have a new life plan that took into account all the changes. She already had more than enough money to disappear for the rest of her life, but that would take some hard thought. She couldn't leave the people she cared about behind, not without a damned good reason.

Too late for some choices, it would seem.

The lecture she was preparing for tomorrow only reinforced the disconnect between her past and present. She loved ancient history and archaeology, and a position as an adjunct archaeology professor at UCLA had turned out to be a good choice.

Originally, Peyton had helped her forge the appropriate credentials to score the position. The school didn't mind that she was so busy with *fieldwork* that she only gave a small number of guest lectures throughout the semester. She addressed packed rooms of students on hidden history scheduled around her digs.

Nobody needed to know they were also tomb raids.

Shay shook her head at the memory. Peyton had done a good job of creating a past for her that excluded her time as a hired killer. She was interested in history's truths but had lied through her teeth to get a position centered around exploring and uncovering them. Funny how that worked.

The surprising thing about the whole experience was that once she had started lecturing, she'd found she really enjoyed it. She was eager to get back into a lecture hall every time and drop truth bombs on unsuspecting college students.

But no one could change the past—not even Oriceran magic, as far as she knew. Her path as an assassin had been set when she'd made her first kill at fifteen, but now, whatever came next was up to her.

A full-time position at a college wasn't out of the question, but she'd have to put aside tomb raiding. It'd be a chance at a normal life, and it wasn't like she needed more money.

Shay took a deep breath and shook her head. It was a fleeting and stupid thought. She might love talking about history and archaeology, but she also loved being in the thick of danger and finding hidden artifacts that required not only quick thinking but training. *I'll never be satisfied just digging pots up from the desert.*

Adrenaline junkie? Maybe, at least on some level. A woman interested in the truth couldn't deny the truth about herself forever.

Shay had spent most of her life without reflecting on why she did something, and instead just did it. Introspection was hard, and not always welcome.

Was that why I decided to take on Lily? Am I trying to do something different with my life? I honestly don't know anymore.

She flipped to a bookmarked page, a chapter titled, *A Consideration of the Puebla Tunnels.*

Shay grabbed a pencil and a pad of paper. Tablets and phones were convenient, but taking notes the old-fashioned way helped her remember things more easily. She skimmed the chapter, looking for useful information for her lecture.

Dismissed as legend for many years, the confirmation by workers of the existence of the tunnels under the city of Puebla in 2015 surprised and tantalized the world. Additional testing confirmed that the tunnels have existed since the founding of the city...

In the years that followed, the tunnel system was regarded as merely an artifact of the colonial history of the city, but excavations that started in 2024 revealed an additional and even deeper hidden tunnel system that predates the main tunnel system by at least a millennium.

Shay took a few notes and read a few more background paragraphs before coming to something else of interest. This was what they were going to want to hear about.

The precision layout and construction of the more ancient system wasn't consistent with the technological capabilities of the indigenous human cultures. Prior to public contact with Oriceran, it would have been difficult to understand the true nature of the tunnels, or they might have been dismissed with pseudo-archaeological claims of ancient aliens. Follow-up research in conjunction with Oriceran scholars has confirmed that the original tunnel system was in fact of Oriceran origin and excavated originally with the use of earth- and soil-manipu-lation magic at the behest of dwarves.

Interestingly enough, despite the confirmation of the fantas-tical nature of the tunnels, there remains a mystery on both Earth and Oriceran about why the dwarves chose to excavate the tunnels. The Oriceran sources claim they lack extant documen-tation on the tunnels, other than a few brief mentions of the ordering of their construction.

Adding to the mystery are claims that, until recently, strange noises could be heard from the deeper tunnels. Additional expedi-tions, both technological and magical, haven't revealed anything of note other than a small number of stray artifacts that suggest the tunnels might have been in use well into at least the opening decade of the twenty-first century.

Shay chuckled. Given what she'd learned from Lily, who was one of her inspirations for the lecture, the tomb raider couldn't help but wonder if some hidden Oriceran magical train used to run in the tunnel system, and once humans started poking around, they'd decided to move to a new line. The existence of magic might be out there, but the magical community still kept plenty of secrets.

I better leave that little tidbit out of the lecture. Lily hasn't betrayed my secrets, so I don't want to betray any that might get people poking around where she lives.

Shay grinned. She'd just play up the mystery. *Everyone* loved a little mystery.

A couple hours later, with the lecture notes well prepared, Shay finished brushing her teeth. She was grateful to be at home and away from any gangsters, gang members, or gnomes. She fell face-first into her bed and let out a long sigh.

She'd been too busy to see James for the last few days, and she missed her man. Calling him might be too clingy. They each had their own lives, and he'd accepted that. So had she, or at least she thought she had.

She snorted. The guy managed to be both high- and low-maintenance at the same time. He was used to living alone and doing his own thing, but he didn't understand anything about women. It made even the simplest romantic conversation an interesting adventure, if not a frustrating one.

Her phone sat on her nightstand, almost taunting her, telling her to call or text James.

"No, if I'm gonna keep being a tomb raider, I need to know I can handle a few days without calling or seeing the man."

The dawn sun had barely crawled above the horizon when Shay found herself in the middle of a park in her tank top and sweatpants. The other members of Free-to-Move, the parkour group she'd joined, stood around, stretching in preparation for their run.

The crane stunt from the night before popped into Shay's head.

She stretched her arm across her chest. "Ever wonder how far you can take all this?"

Aaron, who was stretching his quads on the ground next to Lana, laughed. "Always. Why do you ask?"

Shay considered her words carefully. She wanted some feedback on the awesome moves she'd seen Harry's and Lily's friends pull off, but she had to be careful not to get them too much attention. Admitting that she'd seen anything strange was a bad idea. People were naturally curious—just like she was.

"Just wondering." Shay shrugged. "I mean, imagine jumping off a building, then pushing off while you're falling and catching the metal lattice on a crane or shit like that. Next-level parkour."

Lana shook her head. "Oh, that's just movie stuff. The problem is, people forget what parkour is and what isn't."

"What do you mean?"

"It's about mobility, freedom, and movement. It's kind of a movement martial art, almost. It's not about being a daredevil. There are plenty of daredevils on the net doing stupid crap that I would never try, and it has nothing to do with me not being good enough at parkour."

Shay stretched her other arm. "But it's not like there's no overlap. Sure, half the time we're just running on ground level, but when you're jumping from rooftop to rooftop, it's dangerous. We've all done dangerous stuff that might get normal people killed."

Lana sighed. "What you're talking about goes well beyond that. It's crazy, or magical, or maybe both. It's not something I'd even attempt. It's not about mobility and freedom."

Well, it's about the freedom that comes with escaping from gang members.

Aaron stood and surveyed the gathered people. Everyone appeared to be ready to go.

"Sure," he offered. "It's not that we never do dangerous stuff. It's just that if you start getting into your head that parkour is about the next stunt, you're missing the point, and you're going to get hurt. Confidence is key, but over-confidence is a killer."

Lana furrowed her brow. "I guess there are the Night Spiders."

Aaron rolled his eyes. "They're just an urban legend."

"Night Spiders?" Shay asked.

"I'm not saying I've seen them," Lana began, "but I've heard about them. Supposed to be a group of kids who roam the streets at night pulling off stunts like you're talking about. Stuff no one should be able to do." Lana shrugged. "It's like Aaron says... No one has any video of them, so maybe it's all an urban legend. I'm not sure I believe they are real."

Aaron shook his head. "I *definitely* don't believe they are. If some kids had magic and could do badass parkour, I don't think they'd hide it. No reason to." He gestured and took off at a jog. "Let's get going."

Shay followed, along with Lana and the others.

Oh, they have their reasons to hide, Aaron.

Shay was disappointed that Aaron and Lana didn't seem to believe in the possibility, and surprised that a group of parkour practitioners wouldn't be more excited about someone taking their sport to the next level. If she pressed them on the issue, though, it would only make them suspicious. Anyway, it wasn't like they wouldn't have a lot of time to chat while they were on their run.

I need to push myself harder. Get faster. I need to do more than just keep up with them, I need to be better than them. They might be afraid of that edge, but you can't get stronger until you work up the guts to take the step over it.

Aaron headed straight for a bench and used it to launch himself over a wrought-iron fence topped with sharp points. Lana followed, then a few others before Shay.

Not gonna die from that, but could have still gotten hurt. You're all more into danger than you'll admit.

All of the runners landed with a fluid roll, including Shay. Aaron cut across an empty street and headed toward a narrow alley between two small buildings.

Shay had not run this course with them before and had pointedly not asked about it, other than where it ended. The less she knew, the more she would have to react in the moment, which was better training for dangerous situations.

They might view parkour as a sport or way of life, but she considered it another weapon in her arsenal.

Shay looked past Aaron toward the alley, trying to anticipate possible handholds and sources of momentum.

Window ledges on both sides in case he needs a handhold, only a few stories high. Bet he's gonna head up to the roof.

Aaron sprinted into the alley and charged a wall. He leapt up and pushed off it toward the other. He alternated between them as he climbed the side of the building, and Lana followed. Shay gritted her teeth and rushed forward, passing several club members.

She was tired of bringing up the rear. Even if she was still new at parkour, she'd honed her body into a fine instrument for over a decade. She knew the limits of every muscle and every bone. She could do this.

Shay jumped toward the wall and twisted before catapulting herself toward the opposite wall. She pushed away all thoughts except ascending the building. She hit the top in what felt like seconds and grabbed the edge of the roof to pull herself up.

Aaron and Lana were already almost to the far edge of the roof. Everyone else was still ascending.

Third place, huh? I'll take it.

The tomb raider hurried after the other two, ignoring them as they leapt from the roof and landed on the next. She launched herself from the roof and flew through the air, tucking into a smooth roll at the end. When she popped up, she'd lost none of her momentum.

Shay risked a glance over her shoulder. The rest of the club members were close behind. She'd need to push if she wanted to retain her third-place position.

Her side ached a little, but when she'd checked her wound that morning it was healing well enough.

Another reason to not see James for a few days. Don't want him asking questions about where and how I got injured when I wasn't even supposed to be on a job.

Another roof-jump pushed the thought out of her head, but it quickly returned. Guilt was still a novel feeling for her. She didn't like lying to James, even by omission.

Concealing the truth of the existence of other alien artifacts and the government conspiracy from the bounty hunter was at least arguably for his own good. She was protecting him from a head trip that might cause him to do something stupid against a group he couldn't beat.

Not telling him about Lily was a different matter. Part of it was to protect Lily's privacy, and part was because she just didn't want to complicate things between her and James.

Well, he did try to get Peyton to not tell me about that woman using my likeness and the AET shit.

Shay continued to follow Aaron and Lana. She leapt from the roof onto the landing of some metal stairs and rushed down toward the street. Their heavy footfalls echoed in the morning air.

A few secrets keep everyone happier and healthier. I'm sure someone has said shit like that. If not, then I'm saying it.

Sweat dripped down Shay's face. Running several miles would have been tough, even without all the jumping, grabbing, and rolling.

Shay looked over her shoulder again. Still third place.

This time third, next time second, and soon I'll be the one in the front all the time.

She let any concerns about Lily, James, and her relationship fade. For now, the only thing she needed to care about was moving fast, efficiently, and freely. She embraced the mobility.

Her interest in parkour might have started when Marcus showed her up, but things had changed. She charged across another roof with a huge grin on her face.

Damn. I love this.

Two hours later, steam filled the room as hot water pounded onto her head and shoulders from her shower head. The run had gone well. Even if she'd fallen into fourth place by the end, she'd still proven that her skills had improved.

Would she ever be able to pull off the kind of stunts she'd seen the tunnel kids accomplish? She didn't know. From what Lily had told her, every single one of her friends had a magical heritage, and powers, even if unreliable.

That might have meant they tapped into their special abilities somehow when they performed their parkour stunts. On the other hand, they might just be brave kids who were used to having to run from the police and dangerous criminals. Desperation could accomplish amazing things even when compared to careful training.

Shay rubbed shampoo into her scalp as she listened to the news report on the radio.

"Police are still baffled by a series of recent robberies in the Old Bank District. Although tight-lipped, the authorities have admitted that the thieves have disabled surveillance equipment during the robberies with what was likely a commercial-grade jammer.

"In all cases, the thieves have entered the buildings from top-floor windows, but several of the buildings have locked roof access, leading the police to believe magic might be involved."

Shay scoffed. This wasn't magic. She knew a thief who could move quickly and gain access to the top floors of buildings without any magic at all. The whole thing screamed of Marcus.

She still owed him for humiliating her the night they met. It wasn't like she planned to kill the man. Beating her at parkour wasn't an executable offense, but she did want to chase him down and prove to him that no one could beat Shay Carson forever.

Shay rinsed her hair as she considered her victories and defeats in recent months.

She didn't feel any shame at some, such as having to run from the invisible army in Ohio. Her defeats at the hands of Marcus, Francois Durand, and Yulia burned the most.

Her jaw clenched at the thought of the Ice Witch. Both Lily and Shay had their reasons to take her down. Someday it might be worth tracking her down, but for now, Shay would only worry about the witch if the opportunity presented itself. She didn't ignore revenge, but she couldn't deny it wasn't very profitable.

Don't worry, bitch. I'm gonna find you and take you down for me and Lily's father.

5

The tall bay door of Warehouse Two rumbled and groaned as it closed behind Shay's Fiat. It was time to start her workday morning.

Shay might have an evening lecture at the university, but her morning routine still included her visiting Warehouse Two to chat with Peyton. Whatever she decided about her future plans, for the moment, she was still a tomb raider, and the more money she earned, the more options she'd have.

The occasional magical club meeting might be okay to discuss business, but her warehouses were some of the few places where she felt completely secure.

That's probably gonna screw me someday, but got to go with what I have for now.

She threw open the door of her car and stepped out. The mouth-watering scent of scrambled eggs, sausage, and cheese ambushed her, and her stomach rumbled.

Guess I should have grabbed a bigger breakfast.

A few more steps brought Shay around the corner. Peyton stood in front of a table with a breakfast pizza on his paddle. An unexpected but familiar gray-haired teenager sat close by.

Shay was smiling before she realized it. She didn't know when or if Lily might decide she wasn't interested in being a tomb raider, but Shay was more than happy to continue to train the girl in the meantime.

A dark, cynical part of Shay's mind almost wanted to laugh. She still remembered the times she'd pulled a gun and threatened to shoot Peyton because she couldn't trust him, and now she was happy to see him and Lily first thing in the morning.

Friends. Maybe even a little bit family.

Osiris padded underneath the table and purred as he rubbed against Lily's leg.

Hell, Shay was even happy to see the damned cat.

I'm getting soft. I wouldn't last a week anymore as a killer. Just need to make sure I'm the most badass tomb raider ever to make up for it.

Peyton slid the pizza onto a tray. After putting his paddle down, he waved to Shay. "Hey."

"Hey." Shay walked over to the table. "Good to see everyone here bright and early." She shot Peyton a glance. "Especially since some of us had time management issues."

He grinned. "It's been a while since I've been late."

Lily swallowed a bite of her pizza and shrugged.

Peyton clapped his hands together. "Oh, good thing you're here. I was going to send you a text, but I figured you'd be here soon. I've got a job lined up for you."

"A job?" Shay asked. "Where? And does it involve catacombs or some frozen lake? I'm not fond of frozen lakes."

"No catacombs, and no frozen lake. It's in Switzerland. It's in a forest, and well, you know it's not that cold in Switzerland in late spring." Peyton shrugged.

"A Swiss forest? Now you've got me interested."

Peyton nodded. "Yes. Now, a little background first." He pulled his phone from his pocket and tapped the screen, bringing up an image of a small golden coin decorated with an image of a man wearing a laurel wreath crown. "Recognize this?"

"Ancient Roman coin." Shay frowned. Common treasure hunts were rarely worth it, especially since moving the items forced her into legitimate channels with middlemen who asked too many questions.

"Yeah, this coin was part of a trove of ancient Roman coins found by a farmer a few decades back in Switzerland."

Shay nodded. "And why do I care about some ancient coins that someone already found? I can't easily steal a trove of coins even if there's a good reason for it."

Lily continued to gobble down her pizza. Her face was impassive as she listened.

Peyton slipped his phone back into his pocket. "Our client has already acquired that coin collection, and he found in his audit that it was missing a particular coin he wants. A coin enchanted by Apollonius of Tyana. It turns out he was a wizard."

Shay nodded. "Not a huge surprise, even before Oriceran. A lot of people associated him with magic. So what's the big deal with this coin? Does it hypnotize people or some shit?"

"With the proper rituals, the coin can be used for divination. Allegedly, Apollonius used it to help predict a plague. That actually got him into trouble with the Roman authorities and the emperor."

Shay glanced at Lily, who shrugged.

I guess just because she has divination powers doesn't mean she's an expert on all forms of it.

Shay nodded. "So, divination coin, got it. How come the client's so certain it's still there? It could be in the ground, or in the ocean, or underneath some dragon in Oriceran for all we know."

Peyton shook his head. "The client has received new information with the help of a wizard. They know it's in Switzerland. They even have decent coordinates to narrow down the location."

"Why do they need me, then? Why not just go with the wizard and pick it up?"

Peyton sighed. "That's where things get complicated."

"Complicated?" Shay frowned.

Lily finished her pizza and pushed her plate forward. "Wouldn't get paid a lot if this stuff was simple, right?"

Shay snorted. "You got me there. But the question is, how complicated? A few idiots I can deal with, but it could be as annoying as being dropped into some anti-technology zone where I have to ride a horse and fight a bunyip with a sword."

Lily eyed Shay. "I'm pretty sure they don't have those in Switzerland."

"Who the hell knows anymore? A wizard could have teleported one from Australia."

Peyton shook his head. "No bunyips. At least, I *think* no bunyips. A team of Japanese treasure hunters is on the move. Not a big official firm or anything, and not even real tomb raiders, just a few guys and some guys they hired. The leads are Daisuke Naota and Asahi Yamamura. From what I've been able to dig up they aren't psychos or anything, but they aren't the kind of guys who are going to step aside just because there's a tomb raider poking their nose into it. They are greedy."

"'Some guys they hired?'" Shay asked. "You mean mercenaries?"

"Nah, not from what I can tell. Nothing serious anyway, but the buzz is that they somehow got information on the location from a spell."

Lily shrugged. "Maybe whatever that wizard did for the client made the coin easy for other people to find. Magical resonance and that kind of thing. I've heard of it before."

"Damn." Shay nodded. "Could be. But that means if we're going to do this, we're going to have to hit Switzerland soon, if not immediately."

"Yeah, that's what I was thinking," Peyton replied. "Which is why I'm glad you're here. So what's the call?"

"Book a couple seats on a supersonic for tonight. I have my lecture to deliver, and I'll head out right after that. If we have the coordinates, it should be a quick pick-up."

"A couple of seats?" Peyton looked at Lily. "You're taking her?"

Shay nodded. "Yep. Can't learn to be a tomb raider if she never goes out on tomb raids, and this one sounds low-key enough. I'm sure we can avoid the Japanese guys without trying too hard."

Lily blinked and jumped to her feet, excitement all over her face.

Peyton laughed. "Wow. Don't think I've ever seen you express that much emotion." He shrugged. "Okay, I'll get another set of equipment ready to go."

Switzerland and magic coins might have weighed on her mind on any night, but as Shay finished delivering her lecture to the wide-eyed undergraduates in the lecture hall, she didn't give a shit about the artifact or the raid.

Truth. That's what I delivered to them. Fucking truth. I love it, and they love it. Maybe there's some hope for this shitty world after all.

A petite blonde in the front row raised her hand.

Shay pointed at her. "What's your question?"

The girl smiled. "Well, you talked a lot about how there were two tunnel systems, but most of the legends seemed to concern only the upper human tunnel system. It was basically incidental that they discovered the other tunnel system."

"Yes, I'd say that's an accurate evaluation of what happened."

"Do you think that the legends were fueled more by the Oriceran tunnels then, or it's just a coincidence, and people were lucky to have even found the older tunnel system?"

Shay smiled. "Great question. Yes, in this case, I think it *is* a bit of a coincidence. In most cases of Oriceran influence, there's at least a semi-direct link between the existing lore and the truth. At least the truth as best we know when it comes to the artifact or location, even if it's obscured behind heavily accreted myths and legends. In this case, we were just lucky there happened to be more ancient tunnels. Nothing wrong with a little serendipity in the pursuit of the truth though, right?"

The gathered students chuckled.

Shay moved to her lectern and tapped the tablet. A picture of a smoothly-carved tunnel lit by portable string lights appeared on the screen in the front of the lecture hall. "This is where things get very exciting. Just because we know about Oriceran now doesn't mean that every rumor or legend is true, or even evidence of anything more than good storytelling.

"This is where historians and archaeologists have a lot of work to do to dig, metaphorically or not, into these rumors and legends to discern the actual truth. Then, and only then, can we have a true understanding of what has unfolded on Earth and Oriceran. The more we understand about what might have happened, the better we know what to look for."

A huge undergraduate in the front seat raised his hand.

"Yes?" Shay asked.

He shrugged. "So, you know, everyone's talking about how all this old stuff maybe is Oriceran, maybe it isn't, but they didn't say that before. They used to say a lot of stuff was alien, you know, like the pyramids, but now they say it's Atlantean."

Shay nodded slowly. "That's correct."

"Just saying, how do we know that's right? Maybe

there's like a thousand planets out there filled with elves and crazy aliens, and they've all done different things. We're all just assuming it's Oriceran because that's the easy explanation. Like you said earlier…something with a P?"

Damn. Good instincts, kid. I wish I could tell you the complete truth, but this time I just have to point you that way.

Shay shrugged. "It's definitely a possibility, and one I don't think any responsible truth-seeker should discard. Paradigm changes in our understanding make certain things seem obvious in hindsight, such as Oriceran influence. It's entirely possible that in the future, provided we get concrete evidence, we'll find there are other ancient influences on our world that haven't previously been accounted for." She rubbed her hands together, and her eyes gleamed with excitement. "If you take anything away from my lectures, it's that you should continue to question. The truth isn't what someone says in a book. The truth exists out there, yearning to be found, and it's your responsibility as future scholars to find it, even if it's uncomfortable."

The blonde from before frowned. "Uncomfortable?" She looked at her friend sitting behind her, but the other girl just shrugged, clearly not understanding what might be discomforting about archaeology.

"Yes, uncomfortable," Shay repeated. "Most of you don't get it. You've grown up your entire life with magic being a real and obvious thing—something taught in school alongside history, with elves and dwarves and wizards being something the government had to make laws for." She shook her head. "I was just a kid when the truth came out about Oriceran, but it still blew me away. Everyone had always told me, 'Magic isn't real. It's just something in books and movies.' And then the next thing you know, magic's not only real, but it's helped shape our world, and changed our history and our very understanding of our civilization." She swept her hand through the air, gesturing to the entire class. "You take for granted the wonder that is Oriceran. You take it for granted that everything we thought was true for centuries, if not thousands of years, turned out to be crap."

Scattered laughter filled the room.

Shay grinned. "I hope you live long enough for something else big to shock you and make you question everything like it did me. It's uncomfortable at times to stare into the truth when it goes against what you think you know, but in the end, you'll feel more satisfied."

The gathered students nodded, many with eager looks on their faces. Even the students who'd looked bored at the beginning of the lecture now looked interested.

Do what I could never do. Go find the truth without a dark detour first.

6

Shay glanced at Lily as the rental SUV barreled down the dirt road leading toward the coordinates. Her thoughts flashed back to their encounter with Yulia in Antarctica. Even though they'd both survived, Lily had managed to get her arm broken.

A few regrets crept in about bringing the girl along on the tomb raid.

She's a newbie. She might be street smart, but that's different from surviving on a tomb raid, especially if bullets or serious magic starts flying.

The girl had done well helping Shay take down the thugs in New York, but a tomb raid was a much more dangerous scenario. Lily had probably run into more than her share of criminals in her time on the streets, just as Shay had in her previous career, but the strange monsters and magical beings that flocked around artifacts made even the most vicious mobsters seem weak and ineffectual in comparison.

Shay barely stopped herself from sighing. The last thing she needed to do was inject doubt into Lily's mind.

Don't want to see the kid dead, but she's never going to reach her full potential if she's never put to the test. With a little training, those twitch reflexes could make her unstoppable against traps and people. I don't have any magic, so she could end up even better than me.

Lily smiled a little as she looked out the window at the tall pines filling the area. "It's very pretty here. I'm so used to just dirt, concrete, metal, and glass."

"Yeah, that pretty much defines LA. They stick a few trees in to convince us we still have nature, but it's millions of people crammed together breathing in smog." Shay snorted. Not that NYC was any better.

"Thanks for bringing me. I know you're not crazy about me splitting my time between the tunnels and your warehouse."

Shay shrugged. "We still have a lot we can offer each other. I'm not gonna throw away a good resource just because she's mildly inconvenient at times."

Lily chuckled. "That's one way to put it, but I figured out after what happened the other day that you care a lot more than you want to admit."

"Not saying I don't give a shit, but I'm different than you. You're used to depending on your friends, and I'm used to using people and depending only on myself. A lot of things are new to me and I'm still getting used to them, including training people. This isn't always the safest job, so I need to be careful for both our sakes."

"Living in tunnels and having to scavenge...having to *steal* to survive isn't safe either." Lily stared out the window defiantly. "I need something better...a future. One farther out than fifteen minutes. This is a way to do that. A way to do something useful with my powers." She shrugged. "So I'm grateful for the chance and the training."

Shay glanced at the display on the front console. They were closing in on the coordinates Peyton had sent them. She pulled the SUV off the dirt road, and into the trees. After a few minutes of slow maneuvering, the trees grew too thick, and Shay stopped the car and shifted into Park.

"Okay, let's grab our gear. Should be pretty close to here. I'm hoping this won't take a huge amount of digging, but if we can't find it quickly, we'll see what you can come up with."

Lily blinked a few times. "O-okay."

"What's up?" Shay frowned. "You have a vision? Spill it."

Lily shrugged. "It was mostly just you cursing a lot, shaking your fist at the sky, and yelling at Peyton. I don't know what that means."

Shay smirked. "That's most mornings, afternoons, and nights for me. Guess you can see into the past after all." She winked.

She got out, headed to the back of the vehicle, and popped the back hatch to grab her tactical harness and backpack. She strapped a collapsible shovel to the backpack. She finished by grabbed a metal detector, slipping on her AR goggles, and linking them to her phone.

Lily picked up her equipment and a shovel. "Oh, the glamorous life of a tomb raider. I get to dig in a forest. Yay, me."

"Don't forget you also get to see me yell and curse at Peyton. Don't discount how awesome that shit is."

"Oh, yeah, I almost forgot about that."

Shay reached for her ear and tapped the earpiece. "Speaking of Peyton, might as well let him listen now."

Lily mirrored Shay.

"It's about time," whined Peyton over the comm. The line was filled with static. "Pull out the drone so I can get you a bird's eye view and make sure no one is sneaking up on you."

Shay nodded to Lily. The teen pulled out one of the drones and did a quick check of its rotors and power level. She set it on the ground.

"It's ready, Peyton," Lily reported.

A second later, the rotors whirred to life, and the small black machine rose from the ground and climbed to the treetops.

"Well...crap," Peyton offered. "Not an auspicious beginning, one might say." He said the last in a faux English accent.

Shay frowned. "What is it?"

"I've got a visual on two black SUVs. They're farther down the road, though. No other drones in the area from what I can detect."

"So our Japanese friends are here already, but they've overshot?" Shay motioned toward the forest. "Let's go get our coin before it's too late. Peyton, you keep an eye on them and let us know if they head our way."

"Will do, boss lady."

Shay grimaced. "Don't ever call me that again."

"You're so picky about nicknames, Boo."

Lily picked up her last piece of equipment—two metal divining rods.

Shay tapped an overlay command into her phone, and a pointer appeared on her glasses. Lily would make for a nice backup if she could get her power to work, but on this job, they'd been fed coordinates, and their competition was going the wrong way. Everything would be over before anyone had to rely on magic powers.

They headed into the darkening forest. The alpine trees seemed to grow denser with each step. A few birds fluttered away, but no strange shimmers appeared, nor any bizarre sounds. No monsters or enemies, just Swiss nature.

Shay's stomach tightened. All this tranquility and peace didn't feel right. Lily's vision had suggested that something would piss the tomb raider off in less than fifteen minutes. It'd take them ten to fifteen to get to the coordinates, and from what their information indicated, the box containing the coins would be a couple of feet underground. She wouldn't be able to dig it up instantly.

Don't freak the kid out yet. She needs to see me confident.

"Get off my keyboard, you stupid cat," Peyton growled in Shay's ear.

She snickered. "That's some valuable tactical information right there. Our friends doing anything important?"

"Still driving, but they've slowed down."

"Maybe they've spotted your drone."

"I doubt it. This thing is tiny, and I'm skimming the treetops."

Lily raised her divining rods and frowned.

Shay glanced her way but didn't say anything. "We're almost there. If those assholes seem like they're even gonna look our way, you let me know. I don't know how long it'll take to get the artifact out of the ground. Just hoping it'll only be a few minutes."

The next few minutes passed in relative silence. Peyton confirmed that the other team had stopped several miles up the road and was already tromping into the forest with their equipment. They had six men in total, the two Japanese treasure hunters and four others. Two of the four were large men who carried assault rifles, and the other two, who were equally large, only carried shovels as far as Peyton could tell.

Guess that's the difference between treasure hunters and tomb raiders. These guys aren't ready for the level of heat that can show up on these kinds of jobs. They think it's all about the pot of gold at the end of the rainbow and forget about the rabid leprechaun who might be guarding it.

The blinking indicator on Shay's AR display showed they were at the coordinates, a nice and mostly flat clearing.

"Okay, we're here. Guess we start digging." Shay frowned. She'd hoped the digging site would be obvious, but the overgrowth in the clearing didn't give her any clues.

Damn it.

She turned to Lily. "Guess this is where a little magic tracking would help, after all. You might as well see if you can pinpoint the exact spot to save us some time. If you can't, no big deal. No pressure."

The teen stared down at her rods with her brow furrowed in concentration. They pointed together at an angle. "Something's wrong."

"What do you mean?"

Lily shook her head. "The coin isn't here. I just don't feel it. There's no magical essence here that I can sense."

"But these are the coordinates."

"I've been trying to track the coin the entire time, even though you told me not to worry about it. Practice, I figured, but the closer we got to the coordinates, the farther it's felt. My tracking's working, but I'm pretty sure these are the wrong coordinates."

Shay lifted the metal detector and flipped it on. She slowly stepped around the clearing with it close to the ground.

"I have one question for you, Peyton," Shay began.

"What?"

"Has the other team stopped moving?"

"Yeah, they've stopped moving."

Shay continued walking and swept the metal detector back and forth. "Son of a bitch. Lily is right. These are the wrong fucking coordinates, Peyton." She shook her fist at the sky. "And those assholes probably have the right ones. Thanks a fucking lot. Damn it, Peyton. Shit. Damn. Fuck."

"But those are the coordinates we were sent. The client sent them, and I cross-checked and found another dark web source that was talking about them. This isn't my fault."

"It doesn't fucking matter, because the other guys are about to dig it up." Shay groaned. "Damn it. Are they digging in a particular place?"

"They've brought metal detectors. Four of them are using them. It looks like they're working some sort of expanding circle."

"What are we going to do?" Lily asked.

"We can still salvage this. We're gonna march over there and get that coin."

"You gonna kill all those guys?"

Shay shook her head. "Not unless they try to kill us first, but we don't know if they're near it. The Japanese guys are nice enough to show us at least the general location. Here's what we're gonna do. You're gonna find the damned thing once we're close, then I'm gonna distract them while you dig it up. Okay?"

Lily nodded quickly and took a deep breath. "Okay. I… What if I can't?"

"You can try, and that's all I ask."

"Okay."

"Let's do this, then." Shay tossed the metal detector on the ground, and they both kicked into a jog.

Peyton continued to update them as they closed on the other team. The Japanese treasure hunters and their hired hands were walking in expanding circles with no indication that they'd located the coins.

Shay and Lily slowed as the distant figures of the men came into view. They both ducked behind a bush before breaking away to dart from tree to tree.

"Okay," Shay whispered. "Any visions?"

Lily shook her head.

"Can you trace the coin?"

The girl lifted her divining rods, and they turned slightly. She let out a sigh of relief and nodded. It's still way off. I think about a hundred yards."

Shay grinned. "Close enough. Here's what we're gonna do now. First, Peyton's gonna buzz them with the drone to get their attention. Be really obnoxious about it."

"Sounds fun," Peyton commented. "I can do obnoxious."

"Don't I know it," Shay and Lily muttered simultaneously.

Shay chuckled. "Anyway, after that, I'm gonna get the rest of their attention. Lots of noise and nonsense, but not a lot of shooting unless they want it. Lily, you go straight to the coin, dig it up, and run back to the SUV."

"But what if you need me to back you up? What if they try to hurt you?"

Shay snorted. "I've taken on way more guys than this by myself. We're not gangsters looking to prove shit. We're tomb raiders. The artifact is everything. You concentrate on that, and you let me worry about the rest of these assholes."

Lily nodded.

"Okay, you stay here until I tell you to go. You ready, Peyton?"

"Yeah, I'm ready."

"Wait for my signal."

"Yes, ma'am."

Shay snorted. "Don't call me that again, or I'll pull a gun on you when I get back."

She used the cover of the pines to make her way closer to the other team's vehicles. She was surprised that their guards didn't seem to be doing much to monitor the perimeter.

Should have hired better guys.

"Anything?" shouted Daisuke in English.

"No," replied his partner.

The other men shouted their negative results.

Good. At the rate they're going it'd take a while for them to hit the location based on what Lily said. Just need to lead them away.

Shay wouldn't hold back if the men tried to kill her or Lily, but gunning down a half-dozen men might be a harsh lesson for the teenage elf. Unlike Shay, she hadn't transitioned from professional killer to tomb raider. Maybe the girl wanted to be a different kind of tomb raider. Maybe she even needed to be.

She'll have to learn to defend herself, but wanting to waste Yulia isn't the same thing as me taking down people left and right because they're in my way.

"Okay, Peyton, get their attention."

The distant buzz grew louder and closer as the small drone zoomed toward the area. The men looked up, and the two guards lifted their rifles.

"We've got company," one of the guards shouted. He squeezed off a burst, only narrowly missing the drone.

"Geeze," Peyton shouted through the earpiece. "These guys are trigger-happy."

With the attention of the men diverted, Shay took her chance to rush closer. She stood on the other side of the vehicles just behind the guards. The loud report of their rifles rang her ears as they tried to take down the juking drone.

Nice flying, Peyton.

Shay reached into her harness and pulled out a small dart gun. Previously, she hadn't worried much about taking people alive, but Lily's continued presence on missions reminded her that on some occasions it might help.

It also never hurt to test-drive different equipment.

Since some of her personal investigations pitted her against the government, it'd also occurred to Shay that at some point she might have to break into a government facility, and murdering large numbers of federal agents and soldiers wouldn't be the best way to keep her freedom or her life. Trying non-lethal alternatives on her tomb raids would help hone her techniques.

The tomb raider lifted the dart gun and edged around the corner of the vehicle. With two quick hisses, the gun fired its sedative-filled missiles. As she ducked back behind the SUV, the guards grunted and batted at their necks.

"What the fuck?" one of the guards yelled. "I've got a dart in my neck. We've got a sniper…in…the…woods."

He collapsed face-first to the ground. His partner joined him a few seconds later.

Shay holstered the dart gun, then pulled out a five-franc coin and waved it above her head. It wasn't like any of the men could tell what it was from yards away.

"Looking for this little piece of history, boys?" she shouted.

"Get the coin," Daisuke screamed.

Shay smirked. She wished they were in a city so she could lead the men on a little parkour-fueled chase, but the alpine forest would have to do. She spun and sprinted away, the remaining four men right behind her. None went for their weapons, but from what Peyton had said they didn't have any.

You guys are lucky I'm not a little more ruthless, or you'd all be dead now.

The men continue to shout and chase her. Shay headed in the opposite direction of her vehicle. After thirty yards or so, she had to slow down because the men were falling behind.

You guys need to do more cardio.

Shay let them gain a yard every once in a while as she continued leading them away from Lily.

After a few minutes, Lily's voice crackled in her ear. "I've got it, and I'm on my way back to the SUV."

"Great, Lily." Shay let out a loud cackle.

The wrong coordinates thing was annoying as shit, but this is kind of fun now.

No longer worried about them following her, she cut a hard turn and picked up the pace. The yells of the men grew distant, and soon she'd lost them.

"Do you have eyes on them, Peyton?"

"They are kind of wandering around in different directions looking for you."

Shay chuckled. She hurried back to their SUVs and tossed the franc coin on the hood of one—a little tip for their help narrowing down the location.

Sweating from the exertion, she ran back to her vehicle. Lily was already in the passenger seat, staring at a worn gold coin.

Shay threw open the driver-side door and hopped in. "You're sure that's it?"

Lily bobbed her head. "If it's not *the* coin, then it's another magic coin. She patted a rusty metal box on her lap. "And it was the one in here."

"Works for me. Good job, Lily." Shay started the engine. A quick U-turn had them zooming back down the dirt road and away from the treasure hunters.

"What about the drone?" Peyton asked through their

earpieces.

"Keep an eye on them, and after that, just ditch it. After this payday, we'll be able to afford a new drone or two."

Lily stared at the coin for a few more seconds before she put it back in the box. "It doesn't look like much."

Shay laughed. "It doesn't *have* to look like much, just has to be enough to get the client to pay out. Congrats on a nice successful tomb raid, Lily."

The teen grinned.

Peyton chuckled. "They don't look like they're even trying to follow. I think they still believe you're in the woods." He sighed. "By the way, I didn't want to mention it while you were on the job, but I did some checking into the coordinates."

"Don't care," Shay replied. "It was annoying, but mistakes happen, even with you."

"You see, that's just it. I was checking, and I realized the coordinate data file sent to me had the checksum off."

"Damn it."

Lily frowned. "What is Peyton getting at?"

Shay sighed. "Someone fed us bogus information on purpose, probably someone other than the client."

"But why?"

"Good question. Aletheia has a rep now, and not every other tomb raider appreciates what I've done."

"You're saying it was just someone who is jealous?"

Shay's hands tightened around the wheel. "If I'm lucky, that's all it was."

The conversation died. They had no proof or leads at the moment, but they'd scored the artifact.

What if someone's testing me? And if so, why and who?

7

The next evening, Shay sat at her computer in her bedroom checking a few things. The coordinate-spoofing occupied her thoughts. No one had gotten hurt, and they'd escaped with the artifact. She'd have to be careful on future jobs until she figured out who might be screwing with her.

The harsh truth was there were too many possibilities, which made it hard to narrow down the list: Yulia, Francois Durand, and a myriad of other tomb raiders she'd beaten out for prizes during her new career. For all she knew, Irina the *rusalka* had reached out somehow to teach Shay a lesson about overconfidence in alpine forests.

Someone fucked with me. Maybe it was to send me a message. Those treasure hunters weren't exactly hardened killers, so whoever screwed me with must have known my life wasn't at risk.

Shay had thought when she was a killer that she'd understood the world and its dangers, but she knew now she'd been ignorant. Dangerously, painfully ignorant. Even though everyone knew about magic now, secrets and hidden pockets of dangerous wonder covered the world—pockets that altered everything she'd believed about what it meant to be tough, smart, and dangerous.

It wasn't that she'd stopped believing in her abilities, but now she better appreciated their limits and how the kinds of challenges she might face as a tomb raider could easily exceed her existing abilities, especially if she kept pissing off powerful magical beings.

If I wanted a career where I didn't piss anyone off, I should have been a florist.

Shay frowned. Nope. Even that wouldn't work. She'd probably screw up some mobster's wedding bouquets and end up with a hit on her. At least as a tomb raider, she earned enough money to justify everyone's enmity, and she wasn't dead yet. That had to mean something.

The excitement of history coming alive, even if it involved the occasional monster or magical trap, made tomb raiding addictive in a way that killing never had been.

She'd killed because she was good at it and savored a well-executed hit, but the satisfaction didn't linger like that of a good tomb raid. Now, someone wanted to screw with that satisfaction.

Asshole, you should have come straight at me instead of planting a fake clue.

Shay shook her head and sighed. Worrying about problems she couldn't solve was a poor use of her time when she needed to make sure her solutions to other problems were working.

Her fingers flew across the keyboard as she checked the alerts both she and Peyton had set up to monitor his brother's investigative efforts. Everything had been quiet in the days since she'd Scrooged the man, but it'd be a long time before she was convinced that he'd given up. Killing him might still be necessary, even if Peyton wasn't comfortable with the idea.

Satisfied Randy wasn't trying anything, she stood and made her way to her closet. She accessed the hidden panel in the back wall. Several guns and knives hung on racks inside, along with appropriate ammo. A briefcase filled with cash also sat in the hidden alcove, alongside another briefcase.

If Shay needed to bug out, the money in the case would be enough to sustain her until she could access some of her hidden accounts. Even in the worst-case scenario where all those accounts were compromised, there was more than enough money in the case to give her a good head start on a new life. She might not be able to buy herself five custom warehouses anytime soon, but she wouldn't be eating ramen either.

Shay opened the second briefcase to inspect the jammers and AR goggles inside. Everything seemed fine. Other than a little dust on some of the guns, everything was as good as the day she'd bought it. It was a nice set of equipment for common situations.

She eyed one of the pistols, then her three adamantine knives. Even if she left tomb raiding, it wouldn't hurt to have a few hidden weapons located around her house. She'd been forced from her old place to the two-story brownstone because stupid cartel idiots had shown up in her backyard during a situation that had nothing to do with her.

Sure, I'll always need guns, but will I always need bug-out cash? I've got friends and James and shit now. Maybe there will be a time that I don't need to worry about that kind of thing.

Shay snickered and shook her head. Nope. She didn't believe it. Her life would never get that boring. She wouldn't allow it.

Her phone chimed with a text from Peyton.

The client has paid for the coin job.

Good, Shay texted back.

Also checked, no word from the Japanese guys pointing at you. They only mentioned that they ran into some trouble and had to abandon the dig.

Also good.

Okay, good night.

Good night.

Shay tossed the phone back onto her nightstand. Her current life was far different than when she was a killer. She had friends and arguably even family, but it was no less dangerous.

"Oh, well. Might as well keep at it while I'm still breathing."

A couple of days later, Shay stepped out of her car into the bay at Warehouse Two, yawning.

"I'm bored," she announced.

Even though it hadn't been long since her last job, something tugged at the edge of mind, prodding her to do something more with her time. She was half-tempted to try to schedule some impromptu small-group discussions at the college regarding her last lecture.

If I make too much noise at the university, they'll figure shit out, though.

Shay sighed.

Peyton waved from the office. "You're bored? It's not exactly been weeks since your last job."

Shay shrugged and headed toward him. "Yeah, but I like to keep busy. You know me."

"Just saying, a little downtime isn't always a bad thing, especially for someone as, uh…"

"What?"

"Let's just say your default mood is very tense."

Shay snickered. Couldn't argue with the truth.

She glanced around. Lily hadn't been by since the Switzerland job, nor had Shay heard from her. It was hard not to worry about the girl, given her unusual situation.

I'm not her mom or sister or anyone more than a woman willing to help train her in exchange for help. I should remember that. Maybe it'll make me less stressed.

Counter thoughts pushed their way in right after. Between Alison and Lily, Shay had to accept she had more of a soft spot for teens than she'd ever realized or expected. She recognized her younger self in them, and despite the negative events that had already stained their lives, she hoped they could avoid the dark path she'd walked.

No one should end up in their late twenties worried about whether their so-called friends would shoot them to death in their own kitchen. It was as sad as it was pathetic.

Unlike Shay, Lily and Alison also had magical powers

that could be exploited if they didn't learn how to control them and defend themselves. Alison had the school to defend and train her, but Lily only had Shay to help her. Her friends might have her back, but in the end, they were all just lost kids.

Peyton hunched over his keyboard, furiously clicking and typing with a frown on his face.

"What's wrong?" Shay asked. "Is your brother poking around?"

Threatening Randy would at least give her something to do.

"No, no. Nothing like that. I just was trying to find you work because I knew you were going to walk in and complain like you just did."

Shay laughed. "I'm that predictable?"

"Sometimes. Anyway, I've been hitting the dark web pretty hard to turn up something useful."

Shay crossed her arms over her chest. "You're telling me you can't find any jobs?"

Peyton shook his head. "Nope. I can find tons of jobs, but I don't think they're up to Aletheia's standards. You've leveled up enough that it'd damage your brand if you took penny-ante crap."

"You sound like you're my manager."

He shrugged. "Something like that."

"Okay, there, Mr. Coolidge, what jobs are you saying are beneath me?"

"For example, got a guy in Oregon who wants to hire a tomb raider for five thousand dollars to help him find some rare pottery shards."

Shay snickered. "Yeah, probably spend that much on supplies just to find his stupid shards."

Peyton clicked, then tapped the screen. "This guy is offering twenty-five thousand, but it involves you going into some remote part of the Amazon and he's pretty much guaranteeing you'll be attacked by monsters."

"Pass. If I have to fight monsters, I want at least a hundred thousand, if not a few hundred thousand."

"Exactly. Oh, this is a really funny one. A Japanese man is offering a thousand yen for someone to help him catch a *tsuchinoko*."

Shay furrowed her brow. "One of those snake cryptids?"

Peyton nodded. "Yeah. I had to look it up, but that's what they are."

"And a thousand yen is what like...ten bucks? Is he fucking kidding?"

Peyton shrugged. "Don't know. I mean, the offer was on a legit if shady dark web tomb-raider recruiting site. It's not something you can find just by typing 'Need tomb raider' into a search engine. He did say he'd offer ten percent of gross profits on any money he made from the *tsuchinoko*, including—you'll love this—merchandising rights."

"I think he's about twenty years too late for people to be really impressed with a cryptid." Shay shrugged. "He should ask Daisuke and Asahi for help. They probably could use a thousand yen about now."

Peyton smirked. "Very funny. You're such a bitch sometimes."

"Funny bitch, though." Shay sighed. "And that's what we

have available? Merchandise deals, pottery, and guys who want me to risk my life for less than the cost of the equipment for the job?"

"Yeah, it's all that kind of thing. Everything's really quiet. Not the first time." Peyton shrugged. "But nothing worth you getting out of bed for. That's the problem with being such a high-end tomb raider."

"What about Smite-Williams? He's got to have something interesting for me." Shay rubbed the back of her neck, mild panic overshadowing her boredom.

Peyton shook his head. "Haven't heard a peep from him. Come on. It's not a big deal to have a few days off. You've done it before. I don't get why you care now."

Shay shook her head. "It's kind of like parkour. I don't like losing my momentum, and I have a lot of it built up."

"Something will turn up. In the meantime, go hang out with your friends or call your boyfriend. Eat some pizza and barbeque, or a barbeque pizza." Peyton shrugged. "Have an actual life."

Shay snorted. "Right back at you."

Peyton pointed at his chest with a thumb. "I've got a life and a girlfriend, thank you very much."

His fashion sense, including the pastel jacket with shoulder pads, silk pants, and lack of socks reminded Shay of a very important question she needed to ask.

"She's agreed to go out with you again despite your habit of wearing..." Shay gestured toward his clothes, "well, shit like that?"

Peyton rolled his eyes. "She appreciates my unique style, yes. It's part of her being smart and nerdy-sexy. She can see past the petty confines of common society."

"'Nerdy-sexy?' What the fuck does that mean?"

"She works on computer simulations for physics stuff, including the interface of regular physics and magic."

Shay nodded. "Okay, doesn't sound like a bimbo. I'll give you credit for having some taste, and not being scared off by a woman with a brain."

Peyton grinned. "And I'll even admit she's got a thing or two to teach me about programming."

"Does she now? Guess it's a good thing your ego can handle a smart woman."

He laughed. "My boss is smart and has threatened to kill me several times. Kind of makes my girlfriend seem mild in comparison."

Shay winked. "Just consider it part of your man training." She stepped out of the office. "Keep looking… Wait a second."

She took a few steps toward a table near the pizza oven. The bowl on the table had been scraped clean, but the red-stains around the rim and the sweet scent pointed to cherries.

"For the love of all that is holy and sacred," Shay began, taking another step toward the bowl, her stomach tightening, "please tell me you're not making cherry pizza." She gagged at the sacrilege.

Peyton laughed and walked toward the table. "Nope. I figure I've got this great stone oven, so why not do more with it than just cook pizza? It'll teach me to handle the oven better."

"Do more? Like what, cremation?"

"Ha-ha. Very funny. I mean like pies."

Shay eyed him. "I thought you were going to be the Pizza King?"

"Well, the Pizza King also wants to earn the title 'Pie Prince.'" Peyton shrugged. He snapped his fingers. "Oh, I forgot. We had an overnight guest. I found here her this morning when I came in to cook."

Shay stared at him, though inward relief swept over her now that she knew Lily was in the warehouse. "Came in to cook? Don't you mean came in to find jobs?"

Peyton ignored the question and the look. "I didn't ask her much, but I think something might have happened. Something kind of rough."

"What are you talking about? Something happened with Lily?"

"Yeah. She looks pretty worn out and, you know, *dirty*. I get that she hangs out in tunnels half the time, but she didn't get that dirty in a few days."

Shay frowned. "Where is she now?"

"Sleeping on a cot in the break room. One of the few times I've actually seen her sleeping. I wasn't even sure Gray Elves slept."

"I'll go talk to her. You keep looking for jobs."

Peyton gave a little salute and headed back into the office.

The tomb raider marched down the hall to the break-room. The Gray Elf lay on a cot with a thin blanket pulled up to her shoulders. Her face was covered with soot, and her hands were covered with scratches. Her jacket was draped over a nearby chair and had a few new holes that Shay didn't remember being there the last time they'd seen one another.

Shay pulled a chair in front of the cot and turned it backward. She sat down and rested her arms and chin on the back as she watched the slumbering girl.

Lily moaned, and her eyes fluttered open. She let out a little yelp and jerked up.

Shay chuckled. "Good morning to you too, Lily."

"I'm a...very light sleeper. You just surprised me, is all."

"I could say the same thing about you. Not like I mind you staying at the warehouse—hell, I prefer it—but why are you here? You didn't tell me you'd be coming, and you seemed pretty damned adamant about not staying here the other day."

Lily sighed, and her shoulders slumped. "Because I can't go back to the tunnels."

"Can't go back? Why? I don't understand everything about your little group, but it didn't seem like they were about to exile you because you hang out with me. Harry wanted me to throw jobs his way, and he...uh... Well, they don't seem like they'd turn their back on you easily."

"It's not that, it's... I'm being followed. I needed somewhere safe and secure. Someplace no one would ever think to look for me. Some place that even if someone from the tunnels got caught, they wouldn't know where it is."

Shay frowned. "Followed? By Demon Generals?"

Lily shook her head. "Nope. I wouldn't be so worried if it was just some gang members. No, these guys...they're with the 25K Group."

Shay stared at the girl for several seconds before responding. "The 25K Group? The fucking triad?"

"Yeah." Lily looked down and shrugged.

Chinese organized crime had always had a strong influence on the West Coast, but had suffered in places like Los Angeles in recent decades because of the aggressive expansion of Oriceran criminal groups and hungry organizations like cartels and the Harriken. With the recent destruction of the Harriken and the Nuevo Gulf Cartel, however, opportunities had arisen for groups to expand their influence.

Shay had heard rumors that the 25K Group was poking around in Los Angeles, even if they didn't have a major foothold as compared to their strength in San Francisco and San Diego.

"How the fuck did you get the triad after you?" Shay demanded.

"I just...was doing my own tomb raid. I figured with all the training you've been putting me through and how I was able to knock down the thugs in New York, that I was ready to try something on my own. Something local that didn't require Peyton and drones and studying ancient manuscripts."

Shay scrubbed a hand over her face. "Look, I might not have exactly trained at Tomb Raider Academy before I did my first job, but I had over a decade of experience with... related skills. This isn't a job you can take lightly."

"I know, I know." Lily groaned and laid back on the cot. "I just figured that between my divination and my reflexes, it'd be easy. Kind of like in Switzerland—just grab and run. That was the plan, anyway."

"Okay, let's take a step back. I need to know a few details for context." Shay took a deep breath. "What did you try to take? What did you tomb raid? And how did it end up involving the triad?"

Lily sat back up. "We hear a lot of things on the street, and I heard that some scumbags had this artifact, some magic incense that makes people happy. They'd looted some old guy's house after he died. It's not even supposed to be a big deal, just something worth a couple thousand."

"Some old guy just happened to have magic happy incense? That sounds mighty convenient."

"He wasn't just 'some old guy.' He was a big deal in the local Chinese community. A Taoist alchemist."

"Oh, that makes more sense."

Lily nodded. "I figured taking an artifact from a thief wouldn't be a big deal, you know? I didn't want to get anyone else involved, so I found out where the thief was staying and broke into his hotel room to grab the artifact. But I timed it wrong, and he spotted me. I got away with the incense, but now they are looking for me."

"Where's the incense now?"

Lily closed her eyes and took a deep breath. "I don't know. I lost it when I was getting away. It fell, and it wasn't like I had time to search the area with gangsters looking for me."

Shay sighed and rubbed the back of her neck. "Look, I'm not gonna lie and say I've never grabbed an artifact from someone living, but I usually do it only if I have a good reason. That's the difference between being a tomb raider and a basic thief. If you steal from dead people, they don't come after you." She shrugged. "Well, they don't come after you as much, anyway, and they tend to be less mobile. But if you go after the living, it guarantees some-one's going to be out there and pissed. They'll be looking for you, and hoping to put a bullet in you."

"Yeah, I know. *I know.* I screwed up. I get that, which is why I'm here." Lily shrugged.

"That also still doesn't answer the question of why you thought it'd be smart to take something from someone affiliated with a triad. Risk-reward is another big part of the tomb raider calculations."

Lily took a deep breath. "I...didn't check into him enough. I'd heard he was a bad guy and figured I didn't have a lot of time, so I made the move without getting all the details. After he spotted me and I found out he was with the 25K Group, I came here."

Shay held up a finger. "You don't go into the field on a mission without good info. Hell, I demonstrated that shit to you in Switzerland. There's a lot more to tomb raiding than outrunning someone. Good information can be the difference between a paycheck and being dead."

Lily averted her eyes and sighed.

Shay shook her head. "Okay. I'm gonna have Peyton do some research on the local 25K Group presence. The good news is that the 25K Group's got almost no one in Los Angeles right now, from what I know. They've been poking around because of the power vacuum left by the disappearance of the Harriken and the Nuevo Gulf Cartel, so we're talking a small number of triad members in LA. If we get really lucky this wasn't an official triad job, and they might not have even called it in. That means we're talking a small number of people we have to deal with."

"And if they did call it in?"

Shay placed a hand on Lily's shoulder. "We'll figure this out, Lily. Sure, you fucked up, but we all have at one point. I'm not gonna let some triad fucks get you. I promise you that, as long as you promise me you won't try this shit again until I tell you that you're ready."

Lily nodded. "I promise."

The tomb raider nodded. This was half her fault. She'd obviously not done enough to make sure Lily understood the fundamentals and risks of tomb raiding.

I hope this doesn't end with me having to kill hundreds of triad members. Of course, that might make for a fun date with James.

Shay couldn't help but snicker.

8

A few hours later, Shay sighed as Lily cartwheeled around the warehouse, occasionally jumping off the wall and tucking into rolls. Sometimes it seemed like the girl had more nervous energy than she knew what to do with. Maybe it had something to do with her ability to see the future and her reflexes.

I don't think I'd be all that calm if I were getting visions of the future a lot.

Or maybe it was just the way she dealt with effectively being forced into witness protection in the very non-swanky Warehouse Two.

Peyton's initial dives into the local 25K Group suggested they hadn't called for any reinforcements from San Francisco. They didn't even have a great description of Lily other than "an elf girl with gray hair and gray eyes."

Then again, it wasn't like Los Angeles was crawling with Gray Elves. A few questions to the right people might point the triad at her friends, and triad gangsters were a whole different level of threat than Demon Generals.

A loud foghorn blasted from Peyton's computer.

Shay spun toward the office, her hand reflexively going to her gun. She sucked in a breath and dropped her hand before rushing toward the office. Lily somersaulted a few more times before jogging that way.

"What the fuck was that, Peyton?" Shay snarled. "Do we have a perimeter breach? Just what I fucking needed."

Peyton glanced up from his computer, confused. "No, no, no. Any perimeter breaches would also trip an alarm on your phone. It's a job alert. I added the sound the other day because I was getting bored with the old one."

Shay rolled her eyes. "So, what…a foghorn to announce someone's willing to pay me two thousand yen to recover the *Yata no Kagami* or something?"

"Nope. It's a good job. Two million. Um…" Peyton's face twitched, and he looked away. "They specifically asked for you. Well, you know…Aletheia, and they claim that only someone with your abilities can pull it off."

"Two million sounds good, so what's the job?"

"Um, that's the thing…" Peyton let out a nervous chuckle. "It's unusual, but it's straightforward."

"Spit it the fuck out already."

"Demonic chicken." He shrugged.

Shay blinked. "Demonic chicken?"

Lily laughed.

Peyton nodded. "Yeah, there's a hill, Alcock's Arbour in Warwickshire. It's got a ton of supernatural legends associated with it, but it also has a legend of a demonic chicken that's guarding a treasure there. Some people claim a highwayman who was buried in the hill used magic to make sure his greatest treasures would never be taken."

"And this guy summoned...a chicken from hell?"

"Yeah." Peyton shrugged. "Or maybe he summoned a demon, and it possessed a local chicken. Can't be sure."

Shay stared at Peyton, not believing a single thing she'd heard. "What's it guarding? A magic egg?"

"Um, yeah, actually. It's a magical golden egg, though. It's supposed to have some sort of purification magic."

"Bet it makes a great omelet," Lily suggested.

Shay scrubbed her face with a hand before taking a deep breath, then slowly let it out. "And have people gone after this demonic chicken?"

"A tomb raider went into the area a few years back. They only found scraps of his clothes and a few fingers."

Lily winced. "Gross."

Peyton shrugged. "Maybe the chicken's just looking for a little KFC revenge. The thing is, the chicken doesn't always appear. There's some sort of pattern or something. I don't know what it is, and my research says it's appeared for centuries. What I have been able to confirm is that once someone sees the chicken it'll remain for a few days, and the small door that leads to its treasure is only visible for those days. It used to be years or decades between appearances, but it's been showing up much more often in the last twenty years."

Shay nodded. "Maybe that sweet, sweet Oriceran magical energy flowing back to Earth is empowering it somehow. Assuming we buy the existence of a demonic chicken."

Lily moved behind Peyton and looked at a blurry

picture of a gigantic chicken surrounded by a translucent scarlet nimbus. "I have to say, I never thought the first demon I saw would be a chicken. Do you think demon chickens still taste like chicken?" She snickered. "Probably too spicy."

"You think demons taste spicy?"

"I don't know. Maybe."

Shay just continued to stare at Peyton not bothering to wipe the disbelief from her face.

He held up his hands in front of him. "I swear it's real. I've found multiple images of it from different times. The legend is real, and there definitely seems to be something there. I've also found a correlated increase in unexplained deaths associated with appearances of the demonic chicken. So far, no one's been able to get past the chicken, so no one's been able to claim the treasure. It's just waiting for Shay Carson to come and chop its head off."

Shay shook her head. "I can't believe we're sitting around discussing demonic chickens. This is bizarre, even for us."

Lily laughed. "An English demonic chicken."

"Is that better or worse?"

"Probably more polite than an American demonic chicken." The teen shrugged. "Or at least a French demonic chicken."

Peyton groaned and slumped down in his chair. "It's real."

Shay rolled her eyes. "Stop whining, Peyton. I believe you."

He sat up. "You do?"

"Not like there's not a lot of weird stuff out there, so big surprise. Makes me think of that elf in Mexico. I mean, say you're some asshole demon, and you make it to Earth. If you're lucky, you get an Oriceran or a human, but what if you're not? What if the only thing you can find to possess is a chicken? Sucks to be you. No wonder the chicken is killing people."

Peyton nodded. "You can do a lecture later about the threat of dangerous ancient poultry. The risks of chicken going bad and all that. Win-win."

Shay shook her head. "I can't believe I'm about to say this, but let the client know I'll take the job. I'll get past his demonic chicken and get his golden egg."

Lily clasped her hand together, her eyes pleading. "Please take me. I have to go on a job where we take on a demonic chicken. I have to see this thing with my own eyes."

"No."

"No?" The teen blinked, and even Peyton looked surprised. "You want me to stay here with Captain Fashion?"

Peyton snorted and tugged at the collar of his pastel jacket. "When you're older you'll learn to appreciate the subtle genius of my outfits. Each is selected with purpose and great forethought. They are a type of sartorial art."

"Maybe they are selected with the help of a little color blindness?"

"Quiet, you."

Lily grinned. The grin vanished, however, when she turned back to Shay. "Why can't I come?"

"Because after what happened with the 25K Group, you need to lie low, and you also need to learn a few things from Peyton about what goes into a good tomb raid."

Lily sighed. "Okay, makes sense. I'll try to not be distracted by the horrible fashion atrocities committed here on a daily basis."

Peyton rolled his eyes. "The younger generation never appreciates the wisdom of their elders."

"You're not that much older than me."

"I'm old enough."

Shay chuckled. "Here's the thing—you need some practice, too, Peyton."

"Huh? Practice at what?" He frowned. "I refuse to change my fashion sense."

Shay rolled her eyes. "Tomb raiding, dumbass."

"We franchising this stuff now?"

Shay shook her head. "I had you holed up because of your brother. We've taken care of that, which means you need to start getting more sunlight, and you've already pulled enough stunts that I know you'd do all right on some jobs without me watching over you. The more you get out in the field, the better understanding you'll have of my needs, too."

Peyton nodded. "Okay. So, what did you have in mind?"

"Look through some of those minor league jobs. Find something easy, some small artifact or job worth a few thousand. Go ahead and get it done while I'm fighting the Devil's Own Poultry."

"Won't you need me to provide close support?"

Shay snorted. "I can take a chicken on a hill without having a hacker backing me up."

"A *giant demonic* chicken," Lily pointed out.

"Still just a chicken."

Lily glanced between Shay and Peyton. "What about his job? Can I go with him?"

"Nope. You still have too much to learn. You stay low until I can take care of the local 25K guys. I'll handle them once I get back. I don't think frying this chicken is gonna take more than a day."

Shay's small rental truck rumbled along the worn and cracked road, then a rusty gate in front of her cut off further access to the road. She pulled the truck to the side and stepped out.

She took in a deep breath of the sweet woodland air. The full moon and bright stars above kept the night from being impenetrable, but shadows filled the spaces between the densely-packed trees on either side of the road.

The tomb raider grabbed a small drone from the back and set it on the ground. After a quick interface with her phone, she sent the drone into the air. A giant chicken was the kind of enemy you didn't want to surprise you.

The drone hovered above the conical hill of Alcock's Arbour, legendary grave of a highwayman and now allegedly defended by one demonic chicken.

Huh. If a demonic chicken lays an egg, is the egg also demonic? What happens if I eat infernal scrambled eggs? Would that make me evil? What if I bring the demonic egg into a church?

Shay slowly circled the hill with the drone, looking for some sign of her poultry nemesis. She just hoped the thing didn't talk, too. That would be too damned much for her brain to handle.

A faint red glow appeared on the camera feed.

"You're kidding me."

She magnified the image.

"The chicken. Of course. Half-hoped it wouldn't actually be here."

The soft light of the red energy surrounding the giant bird illuminated its form and confirmed Peyton's images. Her avian opponent was large for a chicken, closing on the size of a decent ostrich. Red feathers and a stark red beak contrasted with its bright yellow legs. Other than the red energy field around it and its unusual size, it looked like any other chicken.

Shay shook her head. Just because it was a giant chicken didn't mean she'd lose against it. It was just a damned chicken in the end. A dumb bird.

She programmed the drone to circle the hill and strapped on the sheath containing her *tachi*.

The magical sword might be overkill, but the chicken had to be difficult to kill if it was still alive after all these centuries. The energy field and size suggested it wasn't going to be a pushover.

Shay advanced on the gate, still marveling that she was about to take on a giant chicken.

Okay, so this shouldn't be so bad. Just need to put a few bullets into him before he gives me infernal salmonella.

The tomb raider hopped the fence and jogged through the open field toward the hill in the distance. The sinister red glow of the chicken guided her through the darkness. She didn't even bother turning on the IR mode of her goggles.

I have to tell James about this shit, but he probably won't believe me.

Shay had armed up with the expectation of a serious confrontation. She carried multiple guns, grenades, the tachi, and her adamantine knives. She hoped she could make a little chicken salad without having to go all out, but didn't want her last memory to be getting her ass kicked by a chicken because she didn't have the right equipment.

About the only thing she could imagine worse than being killed in her kitchen by her friend would be getting killed by a chicken.

A loud cluck followed by a piercing squawk rang out. It even sounded like a chicken.

"Our chicken has some nice lungs." Shay unholstered her pistol. "Time to make some wings. Should have brought some sauce."

As she advanced on her avian enemy, more squawks and clucks filled the air. The chicken didn't move. It stood glowing in the night as if challenging her.

Shay picked up the pace, snickering.

Why did the chicken cross the road? To avoid the 9mm.

She arrived at the bottom of the darkened hill. Her opponent tilted its head back and forth, staring down at Shay with glowing red eyes.

The illumination surrounding the monstrous chicken highlighted a small wooden door right behind it.

"I don't know what kind of magic someone used to summon a demonic chicken as a guardian, but this shit ends tonight." Shay strode up the hill with her gun raised, waiting for the powerful poultry to charge. "You can still run away."

At least it's not a drop bear.

The glowing chicken let out another loud squawk and flapped its wings.

"Just my luck, I get a chicken who isn't chicken. Sorry, but I need the egg you're guarding. And shit, I'll take whatever else is behind you."

Shay fired once. The chicken shrieked and charged, but there was no sign of blood or a wound.

"Fuck." The tomb raider emptied her magazine into the charging avian terror, but it didn't even seem to notice.

The demonic chicken was on her before she could reload. The chicken launched a vicious peck at her, and she raised her pistol to block. Shay released the grip and backpedaled. The bird crunched down and cracked the tomb raider's handgun in half.

"Damn it, I really liked that gun."

Shay sprinted along the base of the hill, and the squawking chicken rushed after her.

"I'm going to put a ton of herbs and spices on you after we're done, you feathered freak."

Shay tossed a frag grenade behind her and kept running. When she glanced back after the loud pop of the explosion, she saw the chicken still chasing her without a scratch on it.

This is such bullshit. I'm being run off by a fucking chicken.

She yanked one of her adamantine knives from its sheath, spun, and threw it directly at the chicken.

The blade slammed into the thigh of the chicken, summoning a loud screeching squawk. Red blood trailed down the wound, and the bird flapped its wings. The demonic chicken made it off the ground a couple of feet before dropping back down.

Guess giant demonic chickens can't fly. Good to know.

Shay pulled out the other two knives and took a deep breath. She could plant a blade in the heart of a human with ease, but she didn't trust that strategy against a giant glowing demonic chicken.

The beast took several steps forward and flapped its wings a few times.

"Come on, you stupid pile of nuggets. Let's end this shit."

Her foe took a few more steps forward and clucked.

Shay rushed the chicken, her knives up. She stabbed for the monster's eyes. A powerful swipe of its leg knocked her back several feet. She cried out as her shoulder slammed into the ground and dropped the knife, a shockwave of pain blasting from the point of impact.

The tomb raider rolled aside just in time to avoid a deadly peck that kicked up dirt and grass. She hissed in pain when the rough movement jostled her burning shoulder. A few yards later she bounced to her feet, ready with one arm and one knife.

"I wish I had a flamethrower, so I could fry your ass." Shay threw her remaining knife, and it impacted the chicken's upper breast with a loud thud.

Blood spurted from the wound as the chicken thrashed.

Shay pulled the *tachi* out of its sheath. She might not be able to swing the sword well using only one hand, but now that her enemy was wounded, she had a different strategy in mind.

"Wish I had a chance to see what a giant chicken looks like with its head cut off, but this will have to do, bird brain."

The tomb raider kept her sword low as she charged the giant, glowing, squawking chicken. Each step jostled her injured arm and shoulder sent a new jolt of pain through her body.

Shay's blade impaled the chicken and passed through its body. She let go and yanked out the knife, stabbing the wounded bird as it thrashed and pecked at her. Another blast of pain shot through her wounded arm when the bird's beak tore through her jacket and shirt and ripped into her arm.

The bird, now bleeding from dozens of wounds and with a sword through its body, stumbled backward. With a final loud squawk, it collapsed to the ground, twitching.

Shay dropped her knife and fell to her knees, gritting her teeth in pain.

Okay. This hurts, but it doesn't feel broken. Think it's just dislocated. I can do this. Shay grabbed the forearm of her wounded limb with her good hand. "One...two...three." She slowly pulled until lightning shot through her body.

Shay fell forward, bracing herself with her good arm and taking deep breaths until the pain faded. Her wounded arm still burned from the laceration and a dull ache remained, but the agony at every movement had ceased.

At least I didn't have to use a healing potion. That damned chicken fucked me up more than the last dozen or so guys I fought.

The tomb raider was unsteady when she rose to her feet. Shay watched the chicken for a minute, waiting for it to stop twitching and thrashing. Not willing to take a chance, she used the tachi to decapitate the thing. She wasn't taking any chances with this one.

Shay shook her head and collected her knives and sword, wiping them off on its feathers. She cleaned her bloody hands off on her coat. She'd have to sneak back into her hotel room without being seen. "I murdered a giant demonic chicken" might not be a believable explanation for some people.

With her weapons collected, the tomb raider advanced on the small wooden door. It was far too small for her to enter. A brass knocker served as the only means of opening it.

"No more angry demonic nugget piles," she muttered. She reached down and yanked on the knocker. The door popped open releasing a cloud of dust and a fetid stench. "Ugh."

Three small leather pouches lay inside. They were covered with dust, but otherwise in decent shape. Shay opened the first one and found a golden egg that gleamed in the moonlight. She picked it up and squeezed slightly. It felt solid and heavy.

The other two pouches were filled with small jewels and a few gold coins. Even if they weren't magical, it was a good secondary haul.

Shay tied them to her belt, spared a final glance for the dead chicken, and shook out her sore arm and shoulder.

"You were a good opponent. Don't feel too bad in Hell if the Devil yells at you." Shay took a few steps and chuckled.

Does a demonic chicken get fried down in Hell?

9

Peyton smiled into the rearview mirror of his rented pickup truck, loving the gray cowboy hat, bolo tie, and black cowboy boots. It wasn't an outfit he'd typically wear, but he'd have to change that going forward.

"I am so rocking this look." He nodded and stepped out of the truck.

Peyton strutted across the parking lot toward Lonestar Pawn and Jewelry, one of the many pawn shops in the city of Georgetown, Texas, and one that had a specific item he needed, according to his research and client information.

The faux cowboy threw open the door. A bell rang overhead, and a mustachioed older man at the counter gave Peyton a quizzical look. The corners of his mouth turned up.

Why is he looking at me like that?

Peyton grabbed the brim of his hat and offered the man a polite nod before making a show of wandering around the small shop and taking in some of the items on the walls and shelves. His plan involved him not coming off as too eager. He didn't need to be an expert negotiator to know that.

"Looking for something in particular, boy?" the owner drawled from the front counter.

Peyton walked toward the counter with a smile on his face. "Howdy, sir."

The man smirked. "Look at you, hat-wearing boy. Enjoying the look?"

"I can assure you that I dress like this all the time." Peyton experimented with a painful Texan accent for the first part of the sentence but had already given up by the end of it.

"Sure, boy. Whatever you say."

Okay, so I'm not the best actor in the world.

Peyton took a deep breath. This wasn't a demonic chicken or sinister catacomb. This was a simple artifact recovery from a shop that had no idea they even had a magical artifact. According to the client, it looked like a simple onyx brooch.

I can do this. Don't have to fight anyone or worry about crazy competing tomb raiders. Simple. Just need to find it and walk out of here with it.

The client said that the brooch had some limited light and fire powers, but it only worked for magical beings. It was effectively just a magical flashlight and lighter, which was why it had passed through several humans' hands in Texas without anyone noticing it was magical. It also conveniently sat in the glass case below the counter.

Peyton pointed at the brooch. "That looks pretty."

The man arched a brow. "Yeah, you could say that. Just got this in the other day. Five thousand dollars."

Peyton managed not to bug his eyes out. The client was only offering two thousand dollars. Shay would mock him for the next twenty years if he took such a high-percentage loss even if the absolute amount was pocket change to her.

"Five thousand dollars? Do I look like some sort of Hollywood actor? I'm a rancher."

The owner chuckled. "Nope. You don't look like an actor, boy, but the only kind of rancher you are is all hat and no cattle."

Peyton blinked, not sure how to respond to that. Maybe he should have kept trying with the accent.

How would Shay handle this? Oh, probably with flying fists and guns, or by breaking in during the middle of the night to steal it. I can do this. Just need a little Peyton elegance.

He cleared his throat. "Because I'm aching for a nice gift, and I just sold one of my prize-winning heifers, I'm willing to give you five hundred for it."

The owner laughed and slapped his hand against the counter. "Boy, you loco or something?"

"That isn't worth five thousand dollars. I know that much, even if I am loco."

"I'll give you that, boy. How about twenty-five hundred?"

Peyton shook his head. "Because I like your face, I can do seven hundred and fifty."

The owner grinned. "I find you funny, so I'm willing to drop to fifteen hundred."

"I can't do more than one thousand."

The other man sighed and scratched his eyelid. "That's me taking a bath, boy."

Peyton shrugged and turned to walk away. "If I'm going to pay much more than that, I might as well grab something that isn't in a pawn shop. She'll just really like that one."

"She, huh? Who? Your mother?"

"Uh, yeah, guess you could say that. Kinda."

The owner pulled a keycard from his pocket and passed it over a reader on the side of the counter. The lock to the glass case clicked, and he slid the door open. "Guess it's your lucky day, boy. I like a man who respects his mother."

Peyton tapped the brim of his hat and nodded. "Much obliged."

The other man pulled out the brooch, chuckling.

Peyton resisted letting out a yell of triumph. Sure, he hadn't paraglided into the middle of the desert or had a shootout with a bunch of Russian mobsters, but he'd pulled off a solid, if low-level, artifact recovery.

Maybe it'd be a stretch to call it a tomb raid, but he was satisfied for the moment being Peyton the Pawn-Shop Raider.

James' F-350 was parked right outside Shay's brownstone when she pulled up in her Fiat. A little antiseptic spray and a bandage had taken care of her beak wounds, but her shoulder was still sore. Her bounty-hunter boyfriend stepped out of his truck and headed toward the garage with a capacious brown paper bag in hand.

Barbeque, I bet. You'd think he would have shown up with pizza, but it's the thought that counts.

Shay snickered and pulled her car into her garage. James ducked inside under the closing door

"Welcome back," James offered as Shay stepped out of the car.

"Surprised you wanted to see me tonight right after a job."

James shrugged. "I know you've been busy, so I haven't bothered you, and you're always staying at my place. I figured we could mix it up. I've read that's a good thing to do in relationships." He lifted the bag. "Brought some barbeque. Thought about going to Vegas and getting some Jessie Rae's, but wasn't sure how good it'd be by the time you got back. Still, this is from a good local place."

Shay laughed. "James, you're the only person I'd know who'd drive hours and hours just for barbeque."

He grunted. "Maybe the only one you know, but not the only one like me in the world."

"I don't think the world could handle two James Brownstones, and I can barely handle one." Shay smiled. "Let's go eat before the food gets cold."

The barbeque wasn't thin-crust pizza, but it did hit the spot. A couple of hours later, she sat on the bed with her man behind her. He was massaging her tired and aching shoulders. Shay had given him the rundown on the job since he'd asked about her wound.

"A demon chicken?" James asked. "Like the kind that lay eggs?"

"Well, yeah, like that, but evil and huge. And bullet-proof. And frag-grenade proof, the little son of a bitch."

"I hate when they're bulletproof," James grunted. "How did you take it down?"

"My knives and the *tachi*."

James grinned. "Good gift, huh?"

"Yes, for the girl who has everything, a magical demonic chicken-killing sword is a must-have." Shay laughed. "But it did come in handy." She sighed at her lover's skillful work. "Speaking of coming in handy…"

"You know if you ever want me to come with you on a job, I will. I don't need a bounty if it's you."

"I'm fine, James. It takes more than a giant evil chicken to kill me." Shay turned around and licked her lips. "But there's a little something I've missed that you could give me." She winked and leaned over to turn out the light. "Just watch the shoulder."

Shay awoke in the middle of the night, her head resting against the hard planes of James' chest. The bounty hunter slept on his back, oblivious to the world. It took Shay a few seconds to realize why she'd woken up: a chiming phone on her nightstand.

She disentangled herself from her lover's arms and rolled toward the nightstand. Peyton.

311. Give me a call.

Shay stared at the phone, having no idea what a 311

was. She crept out of bed and took the phone with her into the next room to call her assistant and personal hacking specialist.

"Sorry to call you in the middle of the night," Peyton answered.

"That's fine. Maybe. What the fuck is a 311, though?"

"I mentioned it to you the other day right before you left. Huh. You must not have been paying attention."

Shay rolled her eyes. "Just tell me what the fuck it is. You're the one who called me in the middle of the night."

"You know, information coming in that suggests a problem, but not like a red-hot emergency."

"And what information is that?"

"I was checking into the 25K Group guys. They are still keeping it local. There are only a small number of them, but they're starting to sniff around and pay informants. I think it's just a matter of time before they figure out who Lily is, or at least who she knows. Then they'll come knocking on the other kids' door with guns."

Shay sighed and rubbed the back of her neck. She heard a loud thud on the other end of the line.

"What the hell was that?"

"Oh, it's just Lily running and doing parkour and acrobatics and stuff. Trying to burn off steam and cabin fever, I guess. Girl doesn't even seem tired. Surprised she slept the other day."

Shay sighed. "Whatever. That's fine, but why are you calling me in the middle of the damned night about this?"

"If you want to catch up with these guys, it has to be middle of the night because that's when they roam the street. Otherwise, you'll be breaking into a heavily fortified building. So if you want to find them, you better get going. Besides, misery loves company."

"What do you mean?"

"If I can't see Amber…"

Shay snorted. "Fine. You're right. Best to handle this shit ASAP. Get Lily ready to meet me, just in case. I'll be on my way soon." She hung up.

She walked back into her bedroom and scribbled a note for James, which she put on the nightstand next to him.

Be back soon. Have a small side job. Don't worry, it's local and easy.

Shay opened her closet and accessed her hidden panel. City jobs made things a little more difficult, and she didn't want to waste time arming up at Warehouse Three. A gun, adamantine knives, and her earpiece should be enough.

She shook her head. No, she couldn't assume everything would be easy—that would be a mistake. After a quick stop at Warehouse Three for a more standard load-out, she'd go have a chat with some gangsters.

Okay, Lily, let's clean up your mess.

10

Shay stepped out of the van onto the darkened street. She didn't want to risk her Fiat being damaged or broken into while she handled the triad members., It also lacked the appropriate modifications the van had to make it immune to one of the devices she needed for her plan.

Killing the men wasn't on the menu. That would only attract even more attention, which might lead to Lily and her friends, or maybe even Shay. At the same time, if the men decided they wanted to kill *her*, she wasn't going to lie down and die, hence the arming up.

Still, the night's efforts would be another test of her ability to engage targets in a non-lethal manner. At least, that was the plan.

"You still have eyes on them?" Shay asked, her voice barely a whisper. The throat mic would pick up her words.

"Yeah, they are one block north and one block west of you," Peyton reported through her earpiece. "Twelve of them are spread out, but they aren't in earshot from the looks of things. They've rousted a few prostitutes, but aren't doing much other than trying to look tough."

Shay cracked her knuckles. "Okay. I'm gonna jam shit so I don't have to worry about them calling anyone or spotting me with drones. Pull your drone back now."

"You sure about your plan? I mean, there's a lot that could go wrong."

"Yeah, I know. If worse comes to the worst, I can always start killing people." Shay marched up the block. "And send Lily with the package. By the time she gets here, I'll be ready for her."

"Roger that. Enjoy your gangster beatings."

"I always do. It's a nice way to let off steam."

Shay touched a silver band on her wrist and waited for about half a minute. That would give Peyton enough time to fly his drone out of range. She pressed a button and activated the jammer.

About seventy-five percent of the streetlights died.

"Okay, not quite what I wanted, so Stage Two it is."

Shay slipped her phone into a small metal case, then dropped it into a pouch on her tactical harness. She pulled out a metal cylinder with several buttons. She wouldn't normally set off an EMP in a city, but it was the middle of the night with no traffic in a rundown commercial district. The only chaos she'd cause was for the triads.

"Here goes nothing." She pressed the button.

The rest of the streetlights died, plunging the entire area into darkness. According to Peyton's research, she'd have at least a few minutes to deliver the pain before some of the backup systems activated and rerouted the power. It wouldn't restore *all* the street lights, but it'd restore enough to make her job harder.

Shay hit a corner and peered around. She spotted the triad members advancing. They were all dressed in black. A few had their sleeves rolled up to display their dragon and phoenix tattoos, and all of them had guns peeking out from underneath jackets.

"Okay, here it goes."

The tomb raider darted into a narrow alley. A quick pop around the corner put her behind the trailing gangster. She slammed into him in the darkness, knocking him to the ground. Instead of finishing him off, she disappeared back into the alley. She pocketed a few large rocks and grinned.

That went well.

The man shook out his bloodied wrist and shouted to his friends. Shay took a deep breath and charged the alley wall. She leapt up and pushed off before twisting and pushing off the other wall, which sent her higher. It didn't take her long to make it to the roof of the three-story building.

I could have killed all of you assholes already, but I'm holding back. Sure, I'm holding back for Lily's sake, but I hope you appreciate it.

Shay resisted the urge to drop a sonic grenade on them. If she escalated the attacks before she had them in the necessary location, they'd start shooting and things would get out of hand. Instead, she hurled a rock she'd picked up from the alley and nailed one of the men in the neck.

He yelped. "Fuck! Someone hit me in the neck."

One of the other men shouted at him in Cantonese.

Shay bit her lip to keep from laughing. She rushed to the edge of the roof and leapt to the next, landing with a roll. She threw another rock into the back of the head of a third gangster before she ran to the other side of the roof and dropped to a nearby landing. From there, she hopped landing to landing and finally back to street-level.

Shouts of mixed English and Cantonese rose. Shay sprinted away from the building of her latest rooftop assaults, then around the corner of a small laundry.

The triad gangsters had tightened their formation, just as she'd wanted. Several had knives or guns out as they desperately searched for the enemy.

"How many of the fuckers are out there?" one of the men shouted.

"At least three," another answered. "Why the fuck are they messing with us? Where are they?"

Shay ran across the street in a crouch, and none of the men spotted her. She ducked in another alley, then sprinted out to slam one of the gangsters' face into a wall before rushing back in.

The triad gangster groaned and shouted something in Cantonese. The twelve men rushed into the alley after her.

Brave guys, but they are doing exactly what I want, so not so bright.

"We'll kill you," one of the men shouted. "We're gonna torture your guy when we catch him. The rest of you better surrender right the fuck now, if you know what's good for you."

Shay continued running. She vaulted over a commercial garbage container with ease and led the twelve men a block away to an alley behind a barbeque restaurant, of all places. She didn't give a crap about the restaurant, but the alley had one important feature—it dead-ended against a nine-foot fence covered with barbed wire.

When Shay hit the alley, she used a metal garbage can as a launchpad to get her to a window ledge, then jumped to the next window ledge until she was on the roof.

She killed the jammer and pulled out her phone. She didn't need to make a call, but Peyton could use her signal to direct Lily to her final location.

The men raced into the alley with their guns out, hungry for their prey. They clustered together, looking for their enemy.

"Where the fuck did he go?"

She, *asshole.*

Shay almost grabbed a frag grenade, but she sighed and grabbed two sonic grenades instead. She tossed both into the alley.

"Look out!" one gangster managed to yell before a high-pitched whine filled the air. All twelve men collapsed, clutching their ears.

The tomb raider dropped down with the help of a garbage can and pulled her gun.

The gangsters remained on the ground, still stunned by the effects of the grenade.

"I've got a gun on you, and I also have the exploding kind of grenade. You can just sit there and rest until a friend of mine arrives, then we can all have a civil conversation."

A nearby streetlight kicked on and revealed Shay's vicious grin to the groaning men.

A few of the men's eyes widened. They'd expected

several people—several men—but instead, they got one very determined and badass woman.

It's almost more fun to do this without killing them, but we'll see.

She snickered.

Minutes later, the gangsters all stood with their fingers laced together behind their heads.

Lily carried a small plastic bag when she jogged into the alley. Once the street light illuminated her face and hair, several of the gangsters growled.

"It's the bitch who stole from us," one man snarled. "You think you can steal from the 25K Triad? No one steals from us and lives."

Several others shouted their agreement or continued growling.

What the fuck? How about a little class, assholes?

Shay fired once into the air. That shut them up.

"I'm trying really hard not to kill anyone tonight. I don't want trouble with your buddies, but at the same time, I can't have you going after this girl. She's a friend of mine."

A tall man with a scarred face who Shay pegged as the leader pointed at Lily. "That little bitch stole from us. Not just anything, but a magical artifact."

Shay rolled her eyes. "That you stole yourself."

"It doesn't matter. All that matters is that she took something that belongs to the 25K Group."

Shay sighed and shook her head. "You know, I get it.

You guys are with a big triad, and your triad has a reputation. You can't have anyone damaging that reputation."

"That's right. You can kill us here, but then our brothers will flood these streets and make everyone you love pay in blood for what you've done."

"Like I said, I'm not trying to kill anyone. The thing is, I don't have a reputation I can scare you with because I'm trying to keep a fucking low profile." Shay gestured with the gun, and her mouth twitched. "But I can still trade on a reputation. I hate to do this, but if you guys won't be reasonable, I'm going to have to take drastic measures."

The gangster leader frowned. "What does that mean?" He rattled something off in Cantonese, and the other men offered a dark laugh.

Shay pulled a business card out of her pocket and handed it to Lily.

The teen took the card and eyed it. "What is this?"

"It's a one-use card. It's got a phone number and some magic. When you use it, the guy who gives out the cards will know your location. The real point is that the guy connected to the card will come if you use it. Read who the card is from for the nice 25K gentlemen."

Lily flipped the card in her palm. "James Brownstone."

Murmurs rippled through the men.

Shay grinned. "Yeah, I'm out of town sometimes, but James usually isn't. You can use that card to help you with trouble." She nodded toward the men. "Trouble like them." She motioned with the gun. "You can drop your hands, but if any of you go for a gun, you all die."

The men grimaced and slowly dropped their hands.

"Anyway, back to the card." Shay sighed. "I hate trying

to ride on anyone's coattails, but shit, if this were tomb raiding, I'd have the rep to push you. Just to be clear, that's a card from the one and only James Brownstone, and I've just given it to this girl you're after. She might decide in a few minutes to call James Brownstone and explain to him that the triads are after her and ruining his city."

The leader's eyes widened, and he visibly swallowed. "James Brownstone? The Granite Ghost?"

Shay winked. "You forget my favorite, Scourge of Harriken." She shook her finger and made a mocking face. "But that's just it. There aren't any Harriken left to harass." She shrugged. "But there are a lot of triad guys he might want to take a crack at. This is a man who traveled all the way to Japan to finish them off. You think he won't waste your asses and take a road trip to San Francisco to kill the rest of you?"

She yearned to brag about her participation in the Tokyo assault, but keeping the men focused on the Brownstone threat would make it easier to manipulate them.

The leader gritted his teeth. "We can't just let someone steal from us and walk away. It'll make the 25K Group look weak."

"I don't even have it anymore," Lily explained. "I lost it."

The man sneered. "Then you must offer restitution."

Shay nodded. She had to give the triad members credit. None of them panicked that they'd been cornered in a dark alley where they could easily be killed.

"Give it to them, Lily." Shay pointed at the bag.

The teen tossed the bag toward the leader, and he snatched it out of the air.

"What's this?"

Shay nodded toward the bag. "There's an onyx brooch inside. It's magic, but it only works for magical beings. You can probably sell it for a couple thousand, which from what I understand exceeds the value of your incense."

He narrowed his eyes. "This isn't the same."

"Don't be a dick. You whined about restitution. Well, that *is* restitution." Shay waved the gun. "You've been paid back, so don't become a greedy fuck now. I'm trying to provide everyone a way out of this shit without anyone getting hurt."

The leader frowned and held up the bag. "And how do I know you're telling the truth?"

"Go get it checked by someone magical. If it's fake, then feel free to keep searching for my friend. But otherwise, you stay the fuck away from this girl. Take your prize and go home, but if you come at her again after being paid back, we'll find a more permanent solution. One that probably involves James Brownstone earning the new nickname 'Scourge of Triads.'"

The men all winced.

Shay backed up, and Lily followed.

The tomb raider gestured with her gun. "Now get the fuck out of here before my finger slips."

The men filed out in a single line, each casting an angry glare at Shay and Lily. Once they were out of the alley they ran off, and a few them flipped Shay off over their shoulders.

Shay let out a breath. "Well, that shit went better than I thought. I think mentioning James combined with that artifact will be enough to keep them away from you."

Lily looked down at the ground. "Thanks, Shay. I don't know what I would have done without you."

"This shit wasn't free."

The teen blinked and looked up. "Excuse me?"

"That brooch was worth a couple thousand, and I just gave it away." Shay holstered her gun and pointed to the retreating gangsters in the distance. "That two thousand belongs to Peyton and it's going to come out of your share of the next job's profits. Everyone earns their keep when they're working for me."

Lily nodded quickly. "I understand, and I'm sorry about all this."

"Don't worry about it, Lily. Just pay it back, and we'll be fine."

Shay spared another glance at the disappearing triad members. She'd bruised and bloodied a few, and they'd probably suffer the lingering effects of the sonic grenades for a couple of hours, but she hadn't killed a single man.

It was an odd experience defeating a gang without serious bloodshed, but the important thing was, they should stop coming after Lily.

The old Shay truly is dead. The old Shay would have wasted all those guys the first minute she ran into them.

Lily eyed Shay. "Something wrong?"

The tomb raider shook her head. "Nope, just thinking about how things change. Let's get back to the van and the warehouse."

11

Peyton whistled as he made his way down the narrow hallway in the physics building with his hands in the pockets of his Nehru jacket. No one even glanced his way. It was as if he were meant to be in a place like this.

Maybe I'm just not that suspicious-looking? Damn. I think Shay's got me thinking in weird ways now.

His stomach tightened as a frowning man in a suit approached from the opposite direction. His gaze lingered for a few long seconds. There was nothing wrong with a visitor heading to the computational physics department, but that wasn't what worried Peyton.

Shay Scrooged my brother, and it looks like it's working, but how can we be sure? Maybe he's just waiting for the right time to track me down and kill me, like when I'm going to meet my girl-friend for lunch. Randy would love to kill me on a date. That's so him.

The man passed Peyton without saying anything, let

alone pulling out a gun and plugging several bullets into him.

Paranoia is not just a river in... Oh, wait, that doesn't work.

Peyton frowned as he continued down the hallway. Randy now knew that his accounts were being watched, so he wouldn't hire someone. If he could figure out where Peyton was, maybe he'd finally take matters into his own hands and finish off his brother. That was assuming he still believed him to be alive.

Randy acted like it, but he was letting greed up his paranoia.

Coolidge family paranoia for the win!

Peyton scrubbed a hand over his face and stopped in front of the door to Amber's office. It might be easier to ask Shay to go kill his brother. She had broken into his house easily enough. Finishing him off without getting caught would probably be just as trivial. It wasn't like she didn't have years of experience killing people and getting away with it.

He groaned.

What am I thinking? I'm going to put out a hit on my brother? Sure, he did it to me, but I'm not a complete asshole like he is. Besides, if Shay thought it was the only way, she wouldn't have gone and Scrooged him. This can work. No one else has to die.

He blew out a breath. The idea of Randy coming to LA to kill him was stupid on several levels, but there was a more important fact to consider.

"Not like Randy's going to be around any smart people," he mumbled under his breath. "Or even semi-smart people."

With a chuckle and a light heart, Peyton knocked softly on the door.

"Come in," Amber called.

Peyton opened the door and entered. The cramped office only had enough room for a small black desk with a computer and a couple of chairs. Although Amber's soft leather chair looked comfortable enough, the other side of the desk had only a stiff black plastic chair.

It's like getting called to the principal's office.

The dark-haired woman frowned as she continued staring at her computer screen. Her fingers rattled the keyboard in a machine-gun staccato. "I'm almost done, and then we can go to lunch. Sorry."

Peyton sat with a shrug. "Take your time."

"You know how programming goes. Sometimes it's easy, and sometimes you just want to pull your hair out."

Peyton chuckled. "Yeah. What are you working on?"

"Oh, a big joint project between the physics department, computational physics department, and the extra-dimensional engineering department. Of course, despite all the people involved, I'm doing most of the heavy lifting on the programming, especially for the testing simulations." Amber grinned, her happy face contrasting with her complaints. "I guess everyone's acknowledging that I'm the best."

"*I* think you're the best."

Amber beamed at him. "Thanks, Peyton."

"So what is it that you're working on? Something cool?"

She nodded. "Simulations on high-energy containment."

Peyton nodded. "Oh? What for?"

"Fusion containment, mostly." Amber bobbed her head and continued typing. "It's not like there's been tons of money for esoteric physics experiments, with everything that's happened in the last couple of decades. And you know, practical fusion—it's always five years away." She finished typing, sighed, and leaned back. "So, step one is exploring simulations of how we might apply magical containment systems to fusion reactions using a special-ized type of air magic that seems to function somewhere between telekinesis and gravity manipulation." She shrugged. "Some of the physics are slightly above my pay grade, let alone the magic, but the short version is that if these simulations go well, there's a good chance the university can get funding for a kind of magically-enhanced reactor that would be very powerful but way smaller and cheaper than other power sources." She smiled. "Lots of papers have come out of the university on the subject, even if they are a little coy on the applications. It's funny how everyone is still afraid of talking about magic even though we know it's very real and powers a whole other civilization."

Peyton sighed. He wasn't solving the energy crisis when he ran down info for Shay or hacked into a few cameras. How lame. He almost didn't deserve a woman like Amber.

"What's wrong?" she asked.

He pointed to her computer. "I'm guessing you're not doing your super-physics and magical simulations on a desktop."

Amber laughed. "Of course not. The department has a dedicated compute cluster for this kind of thing. I access it remotely."

"I've got to admit, I've got tech envy. You have a bigger processor than I do, and your speed is so much faster."

"Well, you know what they say... Sometimes it's not about how big and fast something is."

Peyton snorted. Amber eyed him quizzically.

She doesn't even know, does she?

He shook his head. "Don't worry about it. You're inspirational. Dating you convinces me I need to up my game."

"Not always a bad thing."

"Yeah." Peyton nodded toward the door. "Can you head out to lunch now, or are you still waiting on something?"

Amber clicked her mouse a few times and stood. "No, I'm good. Just been a busy week." She stretched for a moment. "Lots of projects coming together at the same time. Intriguing, but stressful."

"Besides trying to solve the energy crisis, what else are you helping with?"

"I'm involved in a big project with a lot of external corporate funding for quantum-proof public-key encryption."

Peyton stood. "Oh, well, that'd be cool if it were practical. But you know, it's not like the average person is going to be able to beat the quantum computers that the NSA is throwing at stuff. Not heard anything about any companies bringing that sort of thing to market."

Amber shook her head. "This isn't some blue-sky thing. They've already got a working system." She chuckled. "To be fair, it does involve a little magic. I don't know if that's cheating. They've been saying this kind of thing has been close for years, but now it actually is."

"Should you even be telling me this?" Peyton opened the door for her.

Amber stepped through and shrugged. "Maybe not, but you're my boyfriend. Don't want to have too many secrets from my boyfriend, right?"

Peyton smiled, even as a small part of him felt guilty. She shared secrets with him, and he had so many he was keeping from her. Very dangerous ones, at that.

Some inside information about upcoming technology isn't on the same level as knowing aliens other than Oricerans exist and have been to our planet. Or that Shay used to be a killer. I wish I could tell her, though.

For now, though, Peyton didn't care. He just wanted to have a good time at lunch with his girlfriend.

Later that afternoon, Peyton sat at his computer skimming several journal articles that concerned the university's research, along with some journal articles on arXiv, a publicly accessible server covering preprint journal articles.

"Geeze, way to make me feel dumb, Amber," he muttered, as he pursued the abstract of his fifth article. Peyton wasn't a physicist, and the amount of direct computer-related material in many of the articles wasn't as much as he would have liked. Even when he looked up the supplemental information, he was often lost. It was an unfamiliar feeling.

Dating a woman smarter than him was going to take a lot of work if he wanted to keep up. They chatted briefly about the fusion containment project at lunch, and Peyton found himself asking more questions than offering interesting insights.

Hope she doesn't get bored with me, but she seemed really happy to just be able to talk about it with someone. I can always listen. Easy enough.

Peyton's gaze locked on a sentence in the latest article.

Beyond the implications for the energy grid, a fusion reactor of this size could easily be used to provide power for vehicles, and with a few small modifications, space probes and spacecraft. Given the continued expense per kilogram of low-earth orbit (LEO) cargo transfer, reductions in propellant mass have implications toward the future of space exploration.

"I've heard something like this recently," Peyton muttered. "Really damn recently. But where?"

He furrowed his brow as he tried to remember where he might have even read something like that. It wasn't as if he normally spent a lot of time reading academic physics journal articles.

Peyton's eyes widened. But he *did* spend a lot of time doing background research on jobs. It had to be that.

He brought up his browser history and started skimming it. It auto deleted at midnight, but he was sure that he'd read something similar to the article's mention of space exploration earlier that morning.

A few minutes passed as he scrolled, clicked, and frowned after failing to find anything useful. Finally, he found an article from a decade earlier on vimanas and how the ancient Hindu flying machines and occasionally flying palaces might be responsible for many ancient UFO sightings.

Professor Smite-Williams'd had Shay grab a vimana-related artifact, so that settled the question of whether vimanas were real.

Peyton started reading the article.

Many stories about the fanciful technologies purportedly being developed by the Nazi Regime were previously dismissed because of their technological improbability, but with the open acknowledgment of magic, a reevaluation of these stories may be necessary.

He skipped a few background paragraphs discussing the heavy occult influence on many of the high-ranking members of the Nazi regime, along with a history of darker forces on Oriceran.

A few years ago, a previously undiscovered journal of Werhner von Braun was found in Berlin. The controversial German scientist was the father of the guided ballistic missile that was used heavily as a terror weapon against England during World War II, but post-war he was a critical part of NASA's Apollo program. The Saturn V rocket that took men to the moon was designed with his aid and under his direction.

Although the journal hasn't been fully authenticated, it details attempts by von Braun to progress in anti-gravity research inspired by Hindu legends of vimanas with the aid of shadowy forces he refers to only as "the Dark Valkyries."

The journal describes these Dark Valkyries as displaying magical abilities that are fully consistent with what we know of wizards, witches, and Oriceran magical beings. Interestingly enough, the various Earth-based magical beings who did provide aid to the Nazi Regime don't seem to be associated with the anti-gravity project, which strongly implies that the Dark Valkyries were Oriceran in origin, even though thus far any contact between an Oriceran group and the Nazi Regime has been strongly denied by official Oriceran representatives from several races.

Although von Braun's journal isn't specific as to the technical or magical details of what he was working on, he did explain that the key to the project was a "powerful contained-fusion reaction that would rely on specialized air sorcery provided by the Dark Valkyries and would potentially give the Luftwaffe the ability to strike the foes of Germany from the heavens themselves."

Interestingly, von Braun spends more time in the journal later describing the implications of using the technology to colonize other planets and even says the war is "a mere trifle, a testing ground. A spaceship has already been born in our rockets, but they are primitive. They [the Dark Valkyries] will grant humanity dominion over the stars themselves, as is our God-given right."

Questions linger about the authenticity and provenance of the journal given that von Braun's later work at NASA didn't involve similar projects, but many scholars have argued that if von Braun were aware of magic, he might also have been aware of the strict rules concerning magic and once denied the aid of the Dark Valkyries, he didn't want to risk the wrath of organizations such as the Silver Griffins, who were previously responsible for magical control on Earth.

"What's got you so interested?" someone asked.

Peyton jumped out of his seat and spun, startled. Had Randy finally come to get him?

Shay stood in the doorway of the office with her arms crossed and an eyebrow raised. "You're jumpy." She nodded. "Maybe that's a good thing. Never get too comfortable."

He sighed and dropped back into his seat. His heart was still galloping. "Just…was thinking really hard."

"Be careful not to break anything."

Peyton rolled his eyes. "Very funny." He nodded toward the screen. "I think my girlfriend is helping do computer simulation testing work for modern vimanas."

Shay blinked. "Seriously?"

He nodded. "Yes. I mean, she's really on the outside of the project in a support role, but some of the stuff she described earlier lines up with some things I've read about World War II German research into vimanas."

Shay shrugged. "Guess it's inevitable that a lot of the wonders of the past start getting reproduced. Probably only a narrow window to make a good living as a tomb raider. In a few decades, Earth might be as choked with magic as Oriceran."

"Maybe. Just weird to think about."

Shay gave Peyton a funny look. "Huh."

"What?"

She grinned. "Just wondering if your girlfriend might actually prove to be useful beyond booty calls."

"What do you mean by that?"

Shay shrugged. "If she's doing a lot of work with these magical research projects, she might end up having insight into something that could be useful for me down the line."

"I'm so glad you're already thinking of ways to exploit my girlfriend, Shay."

The tomb raider grinned. "Come on, you know me. I'm always looking for an angle on everyone."

The next day at lunch, Bella eyed Shay with a smirk on her face, like she was watching the most hilarious thing she'd ever seen.

The tomb raider put down her huge pastrami sandwich with a frown. "What? Something I need to know?"

Her gaze flicked to the windows. Nothing but normal passersby. Despite all the times Shay had gone out to eat with her friends, none of them had recognized that she refused to sit with her back to the window. She wasn't sure what she would tell them if they finally noticed and asked.

Bella shrugged. "It's just a very big sandwich."

"Langer's is famous for their pastrami, and after running all those stairs, I think we could eat every scrap of food in this place and be okay. I know I'm hungry as a starving horse in the desert."

Janelle and Kara both laughed.

Bella smiled and downed a forkful of her kasha. "You do have a point, and it's not like you have an ounce of fat on you. Sometimes I think after you're done working out with us, you go to the college and just spend the rest of the day working out. Shay Carson, super-athlete."

The university's gym is nothing compared to what I have in Warehouse One, but yeah, you're closer to the truth than you realize.

Shay smirked. "I do dabble in a little bit of extra exercise now and again. Nothing wrong with that."

Janelle took a bite of her modestly-sized turkey sandwich. "Are you addicted to exercise, Shay?"

"I'm not addicted. I just like to keep fit. I need it for work."

Shay managed not to wince. All these months, and she *still* screwed things up by saying too much at times.

"Don't you mostly dig up stuff very slowly with very tiny shovels and brushes?" Janelle looked at Kara, who gave her a quick nod. "Don't have to be that fit, I'd think. Sounds like something you could do as an old woman." She waved a hand. "If this is you worrying about your man, you don't need a man who'll start looking for someone new the second you gain a few pounds. Trust me. Been there, done that, got the t-shirt. Kicked his ass to the curb, girlfriend."

Shay considered that for a moment. Whatever James' faults, he didn't strike her as the kind of man who'd lose interest in her so casually. In everything, he was slow to start, but intense, unyielding, and difficult to stop once he did. Maybe they were more alike than she thought in that sense.

Fuck *opposites attract.*

Shay shrugged. She needed to paper over this with a good lie. "My fitness is just something I need. I've been in…

strange situations on the job. You never know when you might need to hike out of a desert and your phone isn't working."

"That's happened to you?"

The tomb raider nodded.

Janelle chuckled. "Archaeology is more dangerous than I would have thought."

"You'd be surprised."

A young woman stepped into the deli. She looked Shay's way, and her face lit up with recognition. It took Shay a few seconds to recognize her as a student from her lecture the other day, Mary.

The girl waved to Shay and hurried over to the table, delight lingering on her face.

Shay tensed, then let out a breath. She had no reason to be nervous. Students showing up was perfectly consistent with what she'd told her friends about her life. If anything, this would only reinforce the lie of her public cover.

Mary smiled as she arrived at the table. "It's funny to see you here, Professor Carson. I didn't know you ate here."

Shay shrugged. "Not a lot, but yeah, I do."

The student waved to the others at the table. "I'm Mary. I'm studying archaeology and revised history at UCLA. I love Professor Carson's lectures. They are *so* interesting." She frowned. "They are non-credit, too, so it's not like I'm just saying that to suck up to her."

Everyone snickered as they looked Shay's way. The tomb raider shrugged and forced a smile on her face as some of her discomfort returned.

"Revised history?" Bella asked. "What's that, exactly? How is it different than archaeology?"

Mary pulled a seat from another table over and sat.

Thanks for asking, but sure. Go ahead and join us.

Shay cleared her throat. "Well, there are plenty of standard history classes and courses, but revised history specifically tries to focus on areas where normal history was wrong before we knew about Oriceran. It tries to explore both the truth of what occurred in the past and why it was covered up or misunderstood, whereas a lot of times in normal history, they'll just focus on the actual events and the general impact and less about the how and why of the secrecy."

Bella nodded. "Oh, that makes sense. I'm not that much into history, so I guess I don't think about how all this stuff has to be changed now that we know about Oriceran."

Mary's eyes widened. "Oh, oh, oh. I have thought of so many questions since your lecture the other day. Like, how are we so sure they are dwarven, you know? The ancient tunnels you talked about."

Shay shrugged. "Most of that is based off dwarven artifacts recovered from the lower tunnels, along with documentation found by Oriceran scholars and passed along to human academics."

"But Oriceran doesn't quite have the same academic standards as we do. I get that they have ancient records and gnomes and other guys who keep stuff for thousands of years, but it's not like they've been concerned about absolute truth in the way we have been."

Shay's friends continued sipping their drinks and

nibbling their food and watching in silence, but with obvious interest.

This is kind of weird. I've got to turn on my Professor Carson persona. Will my friends think it's fake because I don't even talk the same way I tend to talk to them? Ugh.

"You do have a point, Mary." Shay smiled. "I'm glad you're thinking, and you're right. One problem even with modern revised archaeology and revised history, or related fields such as the history of extra-dimensional engineering, is that a lot of times we're relying on cross-referencing information with the Oricerans, who have a very different frame of reference than human societies do. There are still many questions even on Earth about how the best way is to approach history and what frameworks to use.

"Every historian brings their own biases, even if they are literally just reporting what has been found in primary sources. The sources a person chooses to examine and the methods they use to support them, whether archaeological or historical, heavily influences this in the end."

Mary frowned. "So the Oricerans might be lying?"

"In some cases, yes. Although things like the Great Treaty are masterpieces of diplomacy, the simple reality is that despite the use of magic and the diversity of intelligent species, Oricerans aren't so different from humans. Some are good, some bad. A lot of them have motivations that the average human might not understand, but Oriceran is hardly a utopia." Shay sighed. "The other thing to remember is that it could just be as simple as a perspective difference. An Oriceran scholar or official might not understand the implications of a particular question. They might leave out a piece of information they find irrelevant where as to an Earth historian or archaeologist it'd be considered vitally important."

"I never thought of that." Mary bit her lip and frowned as she pondered the information. "You make it sound like we can never know the truth."

Shay chuckled. "Well, that's not new. Without some omniscience spell, no one can totally know the truth. All we can do is continue to collect evidence and see the general direction it points."

"That's kind of depressing, though." The girl sighed.

"No, if anything, it's the opposite."

Mary tilted her head. "How do you figure?"

Shay pointed to her cup of coffee. "There could be something at the bottom of this coffee that you can't see, or there could be nothing. Just have to keep drinking until we know for sure, but the fact that there's a mystery means it's exciting. I'm interested in the truth, but the hunt itself is exciting."

Janelle, Kara, and Bella all clapped lightly, and Shay's head snapped their way. She'd completely forgotten her friends were there.

Her cheeks heated. Embarrassment. That was rare.

Mary stood. "Oh, I'm being rude. You're here with your friends. I was just stopping by to say hi anyway. I'll see you at your next lecture." She waved.

"I look forward to it," Shay replied.

The student wandered off, and the tomb raider picked up her coffee cup to take a sip and hide behind it.

Why the fuck am I embarrassed? Because I let my friends see there's actually something I care about? It's called having a passion.

Kara grinned. "Your job's way more interesting than I thought." She gasped and put a hand over her mouth. "I'm so sorry. That came out so rude."

Bella and Janelle laughed.

Shay shrugged. "Figured it was just me digging up pots?"

Kara nodded. "Actually, yeah. I mean, I've seen those old Indiana Jones films, the *Tomb Raider* ones, and of course all the Caleb Rodriguez stuff, but I figured that's just movies. Not that my job is exciting, but you're exploring all this weird ancient stuff. Even just reading about it is fascinating."

The other two women nodded.

Just reading about it?

"You have no idea," Shay offered with a smile. "It does… keep me on my toes."

Her friends all smiled as they returned to their lunches.

As Shay's excitement from discussing the past faded, tension suffused her body. She'd been existing in a compartmentalized world: her friends, her parkour group, her tomb raiding, James, and her semi-faux college career. It was easy. It was safe.

Now two parts of her life had collided. Neutral parts that didn't contradict anything she'd told the relevant people, but it didn't change the fact that even in a city as large as Los Angeles, she couldn't depend on obscurity to protect her forever.

Shay kept a smile on her face as she finished her sandwich. The next time it might not be a college student. It might be a Demon General, or someone from the old days.

How can I be careful and still have a life?

As Shay pushed through the throng of people at the mall, her thoughts lingered on the encounter at lunch. There was no question that she was a different person than she had been when she'd started tomb raiding, but she wasn't sure whether that meant she was losing her edge or even if that was a bad thing.

Could someone sneak up on me in this crowd and take me down? Do I even need to be that paranoid when I'm not on a job anymore?

Shay frowned. Yes, she did. She might be an adjunct professor, but that was a hobby. Her main job was still very dangerous. If she ever forgot that she could get herself killed, and possibly Peyton, James, Alison, or Lily.

A little bit of defensive seating and the addition of a few new team members might not save her life. Her friends didn't have to worry about things like that, but if she continued as a tomb raider, it'd only become more important.

I can only compartmentalize so much.

Yulia could have killed Shay and Lily in Antarctica. Someone had screwed with her in Switzerland. The government's lapdog, Durand, knew she was looking into alien artifacts that Project Nephilim and Project Ragnarok sought. Every tomb raid seemed to bring a new potentially lethal enemy.

Not like I ever thought the job would be easy. People don't pay other people millions of dollars for easy jobs.

Shay shook her head and focused on pushing through the crowd toward Prophecy Gaming. The glamour seemed easier to pierce on some visits than others, but she didn't know if that was reflective of her mindset or Tubal-Cain's doing.

She wouldn't put it past the gnome to screw with her for amusement or as some kind of test. Sometimes when she talked with him he sounded like an ancient being who had been forced to lower himself to deal with a mere mortal, and other times he came off like a petty asshole who was more interested in fucking with her than being clear.

What would I do after centuries to keep things fresh? Wait, what the fuck?

Shay blinked. She had spotted the shop, but the sign had been replaced. Prophecy Gaming was now Prophecy Affiliates.

Shay stepped inside. Several soft leather couches decorated the room, along with soft, dim lighting and low oak tables. Various colored crystals floated above the tables and soft string music played in the background, but the harmonies were off to the tomb raider's human ear. Oriceran music, she assumed.

A desk sat along the wall, and rather than a gnome, an overweight, frowning pixie wearing cat's-eye glasses sat there in a tiny chair.

"Do you need something?" the pixie snapped. Her voice was so deep and gravelly that she might be mistaken for James over the phone. The contrast with her tiny size only made her voice stand out more.

Shay looked around, further taking in the startlingly different shop. "Uh, this place is still run by Tubal-Cain, right?"

"Yes. And who are you, and why should I care?"

Shay rolled her eyes. She could punt the pixie across the room, but the gnome would probably have an issue with it. He might be frustrating at times, but he was a good magical contact. She couldn't risk that even for an annoying little bitch of a pixie.

"Shay Carson. I do jobs for Tubal-Cain. Sometimes he makes things for me in return. It's all very useful to both of us, just so you know."

The pixie nodded. "Oh, yeah, you're the tomb raider. He told me you might stop by."

"Who are you? And where's the gnome?"

The pixie arched a brow. "Me? I'm Madge. I'm Tubal-Cain's new secretary."

"Madge? Seriously?"

The secretary snorted and floated off her seat, her wings beating furiously. "What, because I'm a pixie I have to have a name like Moonbeam or Star Flower? You humans. You're all the same. No imagination." She sniffed disdainfully.

Shay shrugged. "Not saying you have to be Star Flower, but...Madge? Come on. You have to see where I'm coming from."

The pixie rolled her eyes and crossed her arms, then flitted around Shay. The tomb raider didn't bother to follow her movement with her head or eyes.

"What kind of name is Shay?" the pixie asked from behind her. "Shouldn't you be Bloody Knives or something?"

Shay's face twitched. She'd accepted that the gnome probably knew far more about her than she'd like, but that didn't mean she wanted any random magical being he associated with to know her past.

But he's the guy with all the leverage in this relationship.

"Why does Tubal-Cain even need a secretary?" Shay snapped. "Is he really that busy? Half the time, the guy's not even in town."

"Again, you're a typical human and assuming the entire universe is centered on you." The pixie fluttered back above her chair. "He's got a lot of clients. Why do you think he's gone? From what he told me, the average human is so slow and ignorant they'll never find the place in a million years, so he decided to stop worrying about faking it being a games store. He wanted something a little more professional-looking. Classier."

"Maybe he should have hired a classier and more professional secretary," Shay mumbled under her breath.

Madge shot forward, and Shay resisted her natural impulse to go for a gun or knife. She refused to believe she'd suffer serious injury from a pixie, whether from arrogance or pure aesthetic desire, she couldn't say.

I'm not afraid of an overgrown dragonfly with an attitude.

The pixie stopped just a few inches in front of the tomb raider, her arms crossed again. "Whatever. He told me all about you. He must really like you because he even told me to let you know where he is if you came in here asking for him." She looked Shay up and down. "You just seem like another human to me, but the gnome's pretty good about exploiting useful *resources*." She smirked.

Shay shook her head. She wasn't going to let the pixie bait her into a further war of words.

"Like I said, I'd like to think we have a mutually beneficial relationship. A little of that makes both worlds go around. Is he even here? If not, I'll leave a message and get out your hair and wings."

Madge's lips pursed for a few seconds. "The Great Treaty."

"What about it?"

"That's where he's at."

"How is he at a treaty?"

Madge rolled her eyes and sighed. "It's a bar. A magical bar. It teleports to a new location every few decades. Been on Earth for a few hundred years, and it's been in West Hollywood since the '40s. Non-magical folks can't see it normally, but they've been lightening up a little bit lately." She rattled off an address. "It's not glamoured the same way this place is, so it's not about just concentrating. You're going to have to go to that address and walk straight through the center of the big mural of Cesar Chavez on the brick wall."

"Won't somebody notice that?"

"Nope. If you're honestly trying to get into the place, people's attention will shift away from you. Just because it's not glamoured the same way as this place doesn't mean it's not glamoured at all."

Shay nodded. "And how do I know you're not just screwing with me and trying to get me to walk into a wall for some sort of Pixie Greatest Pranks thing that you'll put up on the net later?"

The pixie grinned. "That would be funny, but the gnome would get angry with me for upsetting a customer unnecessarily."

And he doesn't care about your attitude? I don't think I'll ever understand Oricerans.

"Okay. I go to that address and walk through the brick wall. Understood."

Madge nodded. "Yes. You won't see it till you're in it. Trust me."

"Thanks. See you around, Madge."

"See you, Shay."

Shay headed toward the exit.

Why do I have a feeling I'm about to break my nose?

13

F orty-five minutes later Shay stood in front of a mural of Cesar Chavez, shaking her head and questioning her life choices.

I swear if that pixie was fucking with me she's gonna pay, Tubal-Cain's secretary or not.

Shay took several deep breaths and stepped forward, expecting a painful encounter with a brick wall and Cesar Chavez.

Instead, the wall rippled like liquid, and a couple more steps brought her into a darkened room.

Okay, that wasn't so bad.

Floating orbs provided light, with a pulsating sphere illuminating a dance floor. Techno thumped from some-where unseen or perhaps invisible speakers. Small black tables littered the area around the brightly lit all-white bar.

If anything, it reminded Shay of an edgy gay bar, except the clientele weren't beautiful men looking for their personal Adonis. The bulk of the bar was filled with the more common humanoid Oricerans one expected on Earth, including elves, dwarves, and a few gnomes, but not Tubal-Cain, from what she could see. There were more than a few obvious wizards and witches.

In addition, many less common beings and races populated the bar. Some were humanoid species that Shay couldn't immediately identify. Many of those had skin of unnatural shades, by human standards at least, from shocking blue to red. Scales. Multiple eyes. Some had pointed tails, pointed ears, or fur. One dark-green woman was covered in vines and flowers that twitched whenever she moved.

Is that a dryad, or do they look different than that?

Shay shook her head. She knew much more about Oriceran that the average person, but every direct encounter with Oriceran culture reminded her that she was still far more ignorant than she would have liked.

Two Oricerans resembling upright elk sat at one table chatting with a roughly humanoid rock being with four legs and two arms. The Oriceran's face seemed to consist of several pulsing gems arranged in no particular order.

So many races. It's hard to imagine growing up on a world where that was the standard for thousands of years.

Shay resisted the urge to twitch at the sight of an Oriceran resembling a giant praying mantis. He rested on a large bench instead of a chair. The mantis chittered away in a language Shay couldn't hope to understand with his seatmate, who looked like an upright rat in a shiny gold coat, huge gold chain, and a large purple hat with a feather, like a little rat pimp.

Huh. So I've finally seen a Willen in person, and apparently they share Peyton's sense of fashion. Maybe he's got a Willen ancestor?

The mantis man, or woman—Shay didn't know which —was downright boring compared to some of the other Oricerans in the place, including a walking toadstool and a pulsing cloud of vapor. She wouldn't have even recognized the latter was alive if it weren't for an elf calling to it.

Wait, how do I even know these are Oricerans? For all I know, some of these are magical creatures who live on Earth and are just now coming out of hiding.

Shit. This place makes the bar I met Correk at seem boring in comparison.

Shay managed to close her mouth and take a few steps forward, surveying the area for the gnome. Being only a small, well-dressed humanoid should have theoretically made him stand out in such an exotic place.

The techno stopped and was replaced by harsh dissonant flute that played jarring, irregular beats. The two elk men bellowed, hopped away from the table, and rushed to the dance floor.

"Must be the song of the summer over there," Shay muttered.

Another vaguely humanoid patron was in blatant violation of local anti-smoking laws, but maybe they didn't count when you were literally a fire. His smoke drifted into the air in a tight column, perhaps guided by some spell. He didn't appear to be burning the chair he floated a few inches above.

Does he have a human shape just to be relatable, or is he naturally like that?

Another quick survey of the bar didn't locate Tubal-

Cain, so Shay made her way to the white bar, which looked normal enough.

The bartender stared down at her. He was a Kilomea—hairy, tall, and brutish, with jutting oversized teeth that reminded her of an ogre.

She'd have to look into it more, but she wondered if Kilomeas might be the source of human ogre legends. It was hard to untangle what magical creatures had existed on Earth all along and which had come from Oriceran. Maybe all of them were originally from the other planet.

Or one of the other alien planets. The more I think about James, the less I can be sure he was originally supposed to be humanoid. Maybe that amulet made him into a human because humans are the main species on Earth.

Maybe it didn't matter. He was all man now. He had proved that to her on more than one occasion.

The Kilomea turned his attention to an older Light Elf in a trench coat. Shay almost laughed. She wanted to ask him if he had baggies of dust or coke in there.

"Another one, Dannec?" the Kilomea rumbled.

The elf shook his head. "I'm fine. I've got too much to do later to drink much more."

The Kilomea eyed Shay for a moment and picked up a bottle.

She understood. It was a bar. She needed to order. She already stood out enough.

Shay sidled up to the bar. "I'll just have…" She frowned as the Kilomea finished pouring a drink and set it in front of her.

"A Lambic, right?" he rumbled.

She nodded. It was pointless to ask how he knew. It could be luck. It could be magic. Maybe both.

Shay took a sip of her beer. "Have you seen Tubal-Cain around? He's a gnome."

The bartender nodded toward a table behind her. She turned around. The gnome sat right there, with a glass filled with a glowing orange liquid in front of him and a smirk on his face.

How the hell? I was looking right at the table only a few minutes ago. Damn magic. Why does it always have to be so annoying?

"How much do I owe you for the drink?" Shay stood.

The bartender shook his head. "The gnome already paid."

Shay nodded and made her way toward Tubal-Cain. Madge had probably contacted him somehow and let him know she was coming, or maybe the gnome could anticipate her actions just that easily.

No, I can't let myself think that way. This guy needed help to find his cousin. He's not all-seeing. He's just old and really smart.

"Hello, Miz Carson," the gnome offered after a sip of his drink.

"Your new secretary's kind of a bitch, you know."

The corners of his lips curled up. "Oh, I know, but she's also reliable and good at screening out the riffraff. Helps me concentrate on my work. Makes the whole operation so much more efficient."

Shay chuckled. "Glad to know I'm not riffraff."

"You aren't, for now." Tubal-Cain gave her a thin smile. "Surprised you'd track me all the way here."

Shay shrugged. "You're sometimes hard to get hold of,

and if Madge is right, I should be happy you ever have time to see me."

"Perhaps." Another sip of glowing orange liquor followed. "So why have you come? You do nothing with me without purpose."

"Fair enough. I need something from you."

Tubal-Cain nodded to the chair across from him. "Sit down and have a drink with me. You insisted on tracking me down on my off-time to talk business, so I insist you play a little."

Shay shrugged and took a seat. She already had a drink anyway. Might as well finish it.

The elk men's song ended. A few seconds later the loud twang of steel guitars sounded, along with a fiddle before the vocals kicked in. It took Shay's brain a few seconds to realize that even though the instrumentation sounded straight Nashville, the singer was squeaking like a dolphin. For all she knew, it *was* a dolphin. Maybe Douglas Adams had been right all along, but instead of being aliens from outer space, they were from Oriceran.

The tomb raider blinked and shook her head. "There's a girl. A teen girl. Half-human, half-Drow."

Tubal-Cain arched a brow. "Half-Drow? How very interesting and unlikely. They are a proud people. If you think *I'm* contemptuous of humans, you should understand how...arrogant they are when it comes to other species, let alone your kind."

Holding back from the man wasn't likely to get the help she needed.

Shay shrugged. "It is what it is. Anyway, this girl is... different. Blind in the normal sense, but she can see energy and souls. I've been doing some reading, and I've heard of magical glasses that can replace or supplement people's senses. I'd like her to be able to both see normally and see energy, or at least see more than she can now."

"It's certainly possible, but it's trickier than you might think. Magic isn't like technology. It's not about just doing the right thing with the right ingredients. Making something such as you ask for might take a while, and it will cost you much more than anything you've asked from me before."

"I've found metal you didn't think I'd find, and I also located a cousin you didn't think I'd find. I'll pay what I need or get whatever you ask if you can produce the glasses." Shay shrugged. "You know I have the skills."

The gnome and the tomb raider stared at each other for a few moments.

Tubal-Cain broke the tension with a smile. "Very well, Miz Carson. I'll see what I can do." He gestured around the bar. "You seemed a little nervous when you walked in."

"What can I say? There's a little more concentrated Oriceran weirdness in here than I'm used to."

The gnome chuckled. "You know what I find interesting? That you find this strange. Earth is strange to me, a planet dominated almost entirely by a single intelligent species. Yes, you have magical beings hiding here and there, but it's mostly just humans, humans, and more humans. It's so...boring. It's amazing that you didn't blow yourself up out of ennui."

Shay laughed. "Well, we've got a lot of different types of humans, at least. That has to count for something."

Tubal-Cain downed more of his drink. "The magic is

back, which you'd think would be a huge change, but for the most part, things are continuing as they always have. You're overly reliant on technology, and your governments are obsessed with controlling magic rather than embracing it and improving your stagnant societies."

"Can't just ignore thousands of years of how things have flowed." Shay gulped some of her Lambic and savored the cherry notes. "Don't know if any of it makes a difference though, really."

"Oh? What do you mean?"

"Like you said, Earth is overrun with humans, and I don't know how much human nature has changed just because of new tools. Magic's just another tool, like technology."

Tubal-Cain set his glass down. "You don't think the return of magic matters?"

"I just know that ancient societies on Earth didn't have computers, cars, or guns, but they weren't all that different from us today. Rich people, poor people. Assholes who get away with shit, and the average person just trying to survive day-to-day." Shay swigged her drink. "The more I look into history, the less I think it repeats itself. It's more that shit just never changes because we've convinced ourselves it has. The trick is for humans to accept that, and then, and only then, can we do something about it."

The gnome nodded. "I can't say that I disagree. It's inevitable, I suppose. Your kind is too short-lived. Humans are always running around in a desperate rush with death hanging over you. It's beautiful in its own way, but it also means that you lack any sort of long-term perspective, and may always lack it."

Shay smirked. "Yeah, don't get too smug there, Tubal-Cain."

"Oh? You were the one complaining about things being the same for humans."

She nodded toward some elves on the dance floor. "Not convinced Oriceran is all that different than Earth. Sure, you've got an untold number of races and shit, but at the end of the day…" The tomb raider laughed and pointed at the ceiling, which she now realized was shrouded in a semi-translucent mist. "This place is called the Great Treaty. You needed that treaty to save your world. Good old-fashioned near-apocalypse. Almost human."

Tubal-Cain snorted. "And it lasted thousands of years. Your treaties are worth nothing."

"Just saying that there are a lot of nasty Oricerans out there, and not just Atlanteans. I think your treaty only lasted as long as it did for the same reason our planet's been able to avoid World War III—mutually assured destruction. The difference is, it took our human asses way too long to develop city- and planet-killing tech, but you magic slingers had it a long time ago."

The gnome smiled, but it didn't reach his eyes. "And now Earth and Oriceran are connected again. If things are as you say, it doesn't matter because even with your people in the know, they are still just humans in the end with all the same foibles."

"Yeah. We are." Shay laughed.

"What's so amusing?"

Shay shrugged. "Don't you think it's better that way?"

"What?"

"That humans are the same. It means we have some

chance of getting through the next few decades of the return of magic without having to throw away everything we thought we knew."

Tubal-Cain nodded slightly and picked up his glass. "I will say this… You're anything but boring, Miz Carson."

Shay picked up her glass. "Well, how about a late toast to not being boring?"

The gnome clicked his glass to hers. "To not being boring."

14

Peyton slapped on a safari hat and stared into a full-length mirror he'd set up in the Warehouse Three Annex. Some people might claim that the hat clashed with the black silk dress shirt he had on, but he liked the contrast in color and texture.

A true sartorial master challenged existing fashion dogma, something his myopic critics would never understand. Besides, it was fun as hell to wear what he wanted without worrying about whether it matched or if it was currently "in."

Lily reclined on the hood of a nearby dark-blue Toyota sedan with her hands behind her head. The vehicle projected more of a soccer-mom vibe than hipness, and Peyton wondered which of Shay's fake identities was associated with it.

Maybe I'll check the documents in the trunk later.

The hacker removed the safari hat and picked up a colorful knit hat covered with repeating patterns. It reminded him of something a person might see in rural Bolivia.

"Hmm, this one doesn't go with this shirt, but maybe the jacket. Plus, I would pay serious money to see Shay wear this hat."

Lily yawned. "You're fooling yourself, you know."

Peyton placed the hat in the rolling rack in front of him and frowned. "I'm well aware of what you and Shay think about my sense of fashion. The problem is neither of you gets that I don't care. It's not like you're the first people to say something about it, and I'm not going to change. A true artist always suffers for his art."

"I live in a tunnel. Fashion's not something I care about." The teen sat up. "So, yeah, not talking about that. Talking about your girlfriend."

Peyton blinked. "Amber? What about her? Shay knows about her, and I know how to keep my mouth shut. If there were a problem, Shay would have already threatened to kill me over it by now. Subtlety is not part of her managerial style, even if she's nicer to you than me at times because you're younger."

"Nothing to do with Shay." Lily shrugged. "I might be younger than you, but I'm not stupid. I also know that girls don't exactly like it when their boyfriends lie to them."

"I'm not...lying to her, exactly. I'm just leaving out a few key details." Discomfort colored his tone.

The teen hopped off the car and went into a headstand. "I'm sure she'll totally agree with your logic once she finds out and not, you know, feel horribly betrayed."

Peyton shook his head. "She doesn't have to find out."

Lily jumped to her feet and stared at Peyton. "Like,

never find out?"

"Maybe. Why not?"

"And you think that's even possible?"

Peyton picked up a red beret and set it on his head. "I was reading an article the other day about guys who worked for the CIA during the Cold War."

Lily yawned. "I'm not interested in ancient history, Earth or Oriceran."

Peyton adjusted his beret. "The point is, these people were secret agents, but a lot of them had families. They lied to their families. Some people didn't figure out their spouses or parents were CIA until years later, or in some cases until after they died. Imagine loving someone and then finding out they weren't who you thought? The point is, if they could do it, why not me?"

"So, because of a bunch of spies who hid stuff from people back in the Dark Ages, you're going to keep lying to your girlfriend?" Lily rolled her eyes.

"When you say it like that, it makes it sound so shady." Peyton grimaced.

"Just saying that shit has a way of coming out." Lily charged a sports car and vaulted over it with three quick pushes.

Peyton shook his head. "But I'm good at keeping things to myself."

The girl turned to face him. "Since when?"

"Since the first time Shay pulled a gun on me. Like I said, not a subtle management style."

Lily snickered. "I can see how that might motivate you." She frowned at a wall clock. "I should be getting home. Didn't realize it was this late already."

"Home? You mean those abandoned tunnels?"

"Yeah. What about them?"

Peyton removed the beret and set it back on the rack. "How can that be a home? It's just…tunnels."

Lily shook her head. "It's so much more than that."

"Roaches? Rats?"

"No. People." She smiled. "That's what home is to me. The people. My friends are my family. We've been through a lot together, and I could never leave them behind. Not totally."

Peyton considered that. He wasn't about to lecture anyone on family, considering his brother had tried to have him killed and his father might have known that would happen. At best, his mother and sister had looked the other way.

Man, is my family fucked up.

Lily looked at the floor and sighed. "Especially since I lost my parents. I had my dad, but he got turned into the bounty hunters by Yulia Solokova."

"The Ice Witch?"

Lily nodded. "Yeah. One and the same bitch."

Peyton blew out a breath. "I knew you had some history, but I didn't know about that. Is that why you're interested in Shay training you? Revenge?"

"A little." Lily shrugged. "That bitch has to pay for what she did to my father. If that freaks you out, keep in mind she's screwed over a lot of people, not just me. I'll be doing the world a favor."

"No, you don't get it. It's not that I care if you kill the witch. It's not like Shay hasn't killed a lot of people since I started working with her, let alone before. It's more about protecting you."

Lily frowned. "Protecting me? That's why I'm getting training."

Peyton shook his head. "You're alive, and that's what counts. Risking your life to protect someone or even for a payday? That makes sense. Vengeance? No profit in it. It's a pointless risk. It will fuck things up, and get you killed. Trust me, I know a little about revenge."

Lily pulled out a small piece of metal out of her pocket. She ran her finger across it like it was a precious treasure.

"What's that?"

"It was my father's. An artifact. It helps me find things. She took it, and I took it back. It's also a reminder that she took him from me."

Peyton had just opened his mouth to say something when his phone chimed. "Hold that thought." He pulled his phone out and frowned. "Huh. It's the Professor, and he wants to meet with Shay. She'll be happy for a big job."

Lily slipped the artifact back into her pocket. "I've got to get back."

"Be careful, and try not to piss off any gangsters on your way home."

The girl waved and turned with a grin.

Shay pushed into the Leanan Sídhe, unsurprised by the dense crowd filling the Irish pub. Just another night at the popular watering hole. Something else surprised her, though.

She took a few more steps before stopping and blinking. Smite-Williams wasn't sitting in the back.

Shit. I'm here ahead of him for once.

The tomb raider chuckled and maneuvered through the throng. She took a seat at a table in the back. A waitress walked over to her.

"What will it be?"

Shay was disappointed that the waitress couldn't anticipate her drink order.

Guess The Great Treaty spoiled me.

"Porterhouse Red," Shay answered.

"Right away." The waitress smiled and headed toward the bar.

Shay settled in facing the front, something she couldn't always accomplish when meeting with the Professor. Just as she got comfortable, the man stepped through the door, gliding through a crowd that parted for him.

The Professor plopped into a seat with a smile. The waitress arrived with Shay's drink and a bottle of Irish Stout for the Professor.

Can't be surprised that she knows what he wants. He all but lives here. Probably has a cot in the back.

"Keep them coming," the Professor told the waitress. "It's definitely a six-drink-minimum kind of night."

She disappeared with a smile.

Shay didn't even bother to talk for the first minute, just sipped her drink as Smite-Williams guzzled most of his.

He set his bottle down. "I'm glad you could come on such short notice, Miz Carson. There's something important I need you to recover sooner rather than later for me."

Shay shrugged. "That's what I do. What's the job?"

"There's a village in England...Ashmore. It's come to my attention that a local legend talks about an actual artifact, a golden coffin that can raise the dead. It's buried in an old stone crypt that the locals avoid, close to the village. It was also protected by powerful wards that have unfortunately faded with the passage of time, which now means the coffin is accessible."

"A coffin that raises the dead? Sounds handy."

The Professor shook his head. "No. It's very dark magic, and the people raised by it become darker, more twisted. Not only that, but it requires a heavy price in the blood of the living and souls." He frowned. "I've also become aware that the followers of a very nasty wizard have a keen interest in this coffin and will be coming for it soon, so you'll need to make a move quickly."

"Who is this wizard?"

"Michael Galbraith."

Shay tossed the name around in her head for a few seconds. "I read that name recently. He's been dead for, what, fifteen years now?"

"That's exactly why his followers want the coffin. To bring him back."

"Makes sense."

The Professor let out a little chuckle. "It might be worth bringing the lad in on this."

Shay shook her head. "James has a visit with Alison. I only wasn't going because I had a few things to research. I don't want work getting in the way of his family shit. We both know he needs to work on his emotional intelligence or whatever the hell you want to call it."

The silver-haired man looked at her with a faint smirk.

"How wonderfully domestic. Very well. I only suggested that because of the unusual level of danger, but I've heard rumors that you've expanded your circle of associates, so perhaps one of them might be of assistance."

Shay eyed the man for a moment. She was never sure how much he knew about her.

"I've got some new friends, yeah, but they don't kick as much ass as James. What do you mean by an unusual level of danger?"

"The coffin is nasty and has the potential to create an undead army, but the forces protecting it are even worse—spectral beings summoned by rather powerful dark magic in the past."

Shay frowned and picked up her drink. She took a sip and set the glass back down. "Ghosts?"

"Of a sort. It's claimed they're soldiers trapped between worlds who've been cursed to protect the coffin." He finished his beer just in time for the waitress to deliver a new one. "So whatever you need to do to destroy them will be fine. You'd be doing them a favor and freeing them from a hellish existence. Oh, one minor problem. They're invisible. Completely."

Shay frowned. "What about if I try looking with tech? Can I pick them up on infrared?"

The Professor shook his head. "An associate of mine scouted the area with a drone. He could see nothing, regardless of how he looked. That didn't stop the drone from being destroyed."

The tomb raider sighed. "I hate invisible armies."

"You've faced one before?"

"At least one, and I've fought more than a few things

that can turn invisible. That's why I asked about using something other than normal visible light." She shrugged.

The Professor grinned. "Wonderful. It means you're a genuine subject-matter expert." He laughed. "How fortunate for me."

"Glad you're enjoying the idea. You said soldiers? So what are we talking? Invisible guys from World War I with machine guns? Angels of Mons?"

"Fortunately, no. It'd be quite the adventure fighting someone invisible who could shoot at you. These spectrals only use swords."

Shay nodded. She could work with that. "And can they be taken out by guns?"

The Professor shook his head. "I highly doubt it."

"You doubt it?" Shay frowned, definitely not liking the sound of that. "I need to know what I'm facing if I'm gonna have a chance of defeating them."

"They've demonstrated invulnerability to rocket fire. My experience in the past suggests when you see that sort of thing it's strong evidence that the creature or being in question is immune to conventional weapons." He took another swig of beer. "But you have magical weapons at your disposal. That should be enough."

"I don't have a magical rocket launcher."

The Professor shrugged. "Something for the future, perhaps. You'll just have to get close and use your blades."

"Easy for you to say."

"You're right, Miz Carson, it is. If I were a younger man, I'd be handling this myself." The Professor shrugged. "Don't worry too much. Even though you've had experience fighting invisible armies, I will note this one does provide one small advantage, and I'm sure you can turn that small advantage into a path to victory."

"What's that? Right now all I'm hearing is I'm going to have to try and carve through a bunch of invisible ghosts with swords." Shay sighed.

The Professor tapped his earlobe. "You can hear them. Their bootfalls, the moans, their weapons. It's quiet, but it's there. You really have to listen, though, and anticipate where they are."

Shay shook her head. "This sounds like bad news. Even if I made James come it'd be too dangerous. It's not like *he* uses magical weapons. You're telling me to go after a bunch of invisible soldiers I can't see but maybe can hear, and who I can't even soften up with grenades or explosives."

"Is that really such an extreme request? You've taken on many dangerous creatures and beings before."

"This is deep shit, and I don't walk into deathtraps."

The Professor eyed her, faint surprise on his face. "A day for the record books, Shay Carson showing fear."

"Caution isn't the same thing as fear." The tomb raider snorted. "And I don't have a dick, so you can't shame me into throwing my life away to prove how big it is."

The Professor guffawed at that. "I will keep that in mind, but let me stress that time is of the essence, and I have few other contacts with your combination of skill and resourcefulness. If the unpleasant wizard I mentioned before is raised from the dead, Miz Carson, it'll cause a lot of complications—the kinds of complications that involve thousands of people dying in horrible ways before he's finished off again."

Shay narrowed her eyes. "And why isn't Correk

handling this? This sounds like something he should give a shit about."

"Oh, I can assure you it is, but he's also unavailable for far less domestic reasons than James. He's a busy elf, and this coffin is but one of many things that threatens the world at the moment."

"It's not like this coffin's the only thing in the world that can raise the dead. Maybe you should worry more about the cult than the coffin. Kill them off and no dark wizard, right?"

The Professor finished his drink and nodded. "I'm quite concerned with the cult, but it'll take time to gather the resources and people needed to finish them off. I won't bore you with the details, but because of the spells used to kill the wizard to begin with, this coffin is actually one of the few ways to bring him back." He tilted his head. "Oh, and I'm willing to pay three times as much as for your last job for me. Consider it a combination of hazard pay and an expediting fee."

"Can't use money if I'm dead." Shay shrugged.

"Which is why I'm willing to pay so much." The waitress arrived with a new bottle even though Shay hadn't even seen Smite-Williams look her way. He picked up the bottle with a broad smile. "Come, Miz Carson. You can help save lives and make a lot of money."

Three times? Damn. That's a lot of money, and the Professor wouldn't give me a job that was a suicide run, if only because he knows James would rip him apart.

Shay sighed. "Fine. I'll do it."

15

Shay stared at her weapons rack in Warehouse Five. The Masamune *tachi* was an obvious choice to fight sword-wielding ghosts. The blade might be her only way of defeating the enemy. Going after them with knives played to their reach advantage.

She'd collected a decent number of artifacts, but she still lacked in quality gear for all occasions.

Need to start doing raids just to pick up gear. Always giving away the good stuff. It's like I'm half-afraid to store too many artifacts here.

She let out a long sigh. Poison-filtering cups and magical lockpicks wouldn't help her defeat an invisible army of spectral swordsmen, and from what the Professor had told her, she wouldn't be able to rely on technology to detect the enemy. That wasn't exactly a minor hurdle.

Shay needed a different solution, some way to track the enemy. She had the weapon. She just needed the eyes.

Maybe, just maybe...

She sucked in a breath. Lily's divination could help her pinpoint the enemy. If it were working well, it'd be trivial for the tomb raider to cut down the invisible swordsmen, and neither of them would be in real jeopardy. If her powers failed, though, Shay would be responsible for the girl being in unnecessary danger. Then again, unnecessary danger was practically the definition of what it meant to be a tomb raider.

Shay shook her head. Lily was her best bet, and if the Professor wasn't blowing smoke up her ass, she didn't have time to fool around trying to figure out the best way to handle the invisible guardians.

"Okay, this is probably a terrible idea, but it's the best one I have."

She whipped out her phone and called Peyton.

"What's up?" the hacker answered.

"I need you to get gear ready for me. Two sets, and get me two tickets on a supersonic to England, along with a rental vehicle that has reasonable cargo capacity. I need to go to a village called Ashmore."

Peyton chuckled. "England, again? Got more demon poultry to take out? Its cousin challenge you to do a duel?"

"Nah, something more basic. This time it's against an invisible army of swordsmen for control of a magic resurrection coffin."

"Well, as long as it's something normal and not overpowered chickens." Peyton chuckled. "Two sets, though? Lily coming?"

"That's the plan. She there right now? If so, let her know I need to talk with her."

"Nope. She went back to the tunnels."

"Okay, thanks. I'll stop by there. Talk to you later."

Shay hung up and grimaced. She didn't have time to wander through subterranean Los Angeles to find the teen, but maybe she'd get lucky.

She tried to dial the girl, but after several rings, the call went to voicemail. That didn't surprise Shay. Tunnels deep under the ground had proven to not have cell phone coverage.

I hope she's somewhere near the entrance and not in the middle of some maze fighting a minotaur. We don't have time to mess around.

"This is a bad idea," Shay muttered as she stepped into the huge pipe. She had a pretty good notion of how to navigate to where Harry had performed his bird calls, but a pretty good notion wasn't the same thing as certainty.

Her wrist light cut through the darkness as she pushed deeper into the tunnels, looking for any sign of movement, two-legged or otherwise.

Funny how this place puts me more on edge than the damned cursed ancient tombs I've actually raided. Those kids survive in these tunnels just fine, so they can't be that bad. And rats aren't a big deal. Not like they can take a bullet like a frogman or invisible swordsman ghost.

The tomb raider walked deeper into the tunnels and turned at what she hoped was a familiar junction. A few more minutes of travel had her questioning whether she'd made a wrong turn. Everything looked the same. Shouldn't there have been some sort of numbers or something?

Damn, these kids have memorized these layouts without any real landmarks that I can see. Impressive. They could do a lot if they got out of the tunnels and just settled down to something approaching a normal life. They are smart and resourceful.

Shay burst out in laughter, the sound echoing in the tunnel. What did *she* know about normal life? She was a tomb raider who used to be a professional killer, and she was dating an alien. Compared to her, a bunch of magical orphans who called these tunnels 'home' was the definition of normal.

Wait a second.

"Fuck." She stopped and looked at the different tunnels leading off from her current junction.

I think I know where I am, but damned if I know where to go from here. This was a dumbass plan.

Shay took a breath and raised her fingers to her mouth. It was time to try what Lily had taught her. The bird call came out half-strangled, but at least she managed decent volume. She tried a few more times, then crossed her arms and waited.

The scuffle of footfalls and murmurs came from a nearby tunnel. Shay didn't go for her gun. The last thing the tunnel kids needed was to think she'd pull a gun on them without good cause. She'd earned their trust, and she didn't want to squander it by overreacting.

The footfalls grew closer, and Harry emerged from a tunnel, followed by Lily, Casey, and a few other teens.

Harry offered a polite nod to Shay, but it was Lily who stepped forward.

"What did you need, Shay?" Lily asked, confusion on

her face. "I'm guessing it's important if you'd come to the tunnels and use that call to get our attention."

Shay nodded. "Have a job, and I need your help. I have to recover an artifact, but it's guarded by an invisible army that technology can't detect. I don't have a decent magical means to spot them either."

"And you think my divination will help?"

"Yeah. You're perfect for the job, but I'll be honest—this shit might get dangerous. I want you to know that up front."

Lily snorted. "And taking on the Ice Witch wasn't dangerous?"

Harry frowned and crossed his arms, but he didn't say anything.

Just stay out of it, kid. I know you're into her, but it's her decision to make. No one likes an overbearing man.

Harry shook his head. "If it's so dangerous, why not bring more backup? The more eyes, the better. We could help." He gestured around. "All of us."

"Didn't you hear me? The army's invisible. Eyes are useless. You can hear them, but that's about it."

He shrugged. "Fine. The more ears, the better."

Shay shook her head. "No can do, ki...Harry. Tomb raiding isn't like stealing from a few Demon Generals, especially when we're talking magical guardians. You wouldn't be more ears. You'd just be more targets."

"We have magic."

"You have *unreliable* magic."

Harry squared his shoulders. "And what do *you* have?"

Shay smirked. "A magic sword that I've used to kill several magical creatures. So I'm good."

Harry blinked. He obviously hadn't been expecting that response.

Lily patted him on the arm. "It'll be okay. I can take care of myself, and Shay can kick ass. She's proven that to us and then some."

Shay nodded. "Look, Harry, I can't be responsible for all of you. This isn't a local job. Your knowledge of Los Angeles and the tunnels would be useless. It's going to be in the middle of a field near a forest, not a city, so your movement skills would be useless." She gestured to Lily. "And I've been training her."

Harry shook his head. "I don't like the idea of her doing something so dangerous by herself."

The other teens nodded in agreement.

"She won't be doing this by herself," Shay countered. "I'm doing the heavy lifting. I just need her to point, and I'll slice." She glanced at Lily. "Like I said, I'm not gonna bullshit and claim there's no danger, though. It's your choice."

Lily nodded, a determined look on her face. "It's time for me to pay back the two thousand I owe. If it hadn't been for you and Peyton, those Triad guys might have tracked me down or hurt my friends. You cleaned up for me when I made a mistake, and I don't forget that. And I haven't forgotten how you helped us with the Demon Generals."

Shay grinned. "If we pull this off, your share will be a lot more than two thousand."

At least we're doing this in the middle of the day," Lily mumbled as she stepped out of the truck.

Shay laughed. "Yep. No reason to make this shit harder than it already is, but maybe we'll get lucky. See anything, Peyton?"

"Nope," he replied through their earbuds. "I'm searching on UV, visible, and IR. Minor temperature differences, but nothing else. Certainly nothing that looks like an army of ghosts."

The tomb raider stared at the simple stone crypt. At ten feet long by eight feet wide, it wasn't all that large. There were no decorations on the outside except a carving of an oak tree on the front door.

Thirteen stones were evenly spaced around the crypt, all thirteen yards away by her estimate. All had large runes that appeared to have been burned into them.

Scorched patches of land peppered the inside of the runestone circle. The glint of sunlight on shell casings from outside and inside caught Shay's attention, along with the dark stains on some of the stones and surviving grass. There'd been a battle here recently.

Your friends, Professor?

Shay knelt near the closest stone. "These must be the wards the Professor mentioned. Said they don't work anymore. Lucky us. Or *un*lucky us, depending on how you look at things."

Lily glanced around with a pensive expression on her face.

"Anything?

Lily shook her head. "No."

"That could be good."

"I'm... No. I just don't think my power is working right now." Lily sighed.

"Don't worry about it. You're doing fine."

Lily nodded, a slight smile returning.

Shay shrugged and walked back over to the squat moving truck. She strapped on the sword belt containing the *tachi.* "Don't have a magic sword for you, and I don't want you trying to take on invisible swordsmen with a knife, so just stay close to me if anything happens."

"Okay."

The tomb raider moved to the cargo door and opened the back hatch. She grabbed a few crowbars and extended a ramp from the back to the ground then pulled the hand truck out. It dropped to the ground with a thud.

Shay pointed inside. "Got rope and a few other things to play with to get the coffin onto the hand truck. We might wish James was here when we have to move the coffin, but once we get it on the hand truck we're golden." She snorted. "No pun intended."

"I'd help you move it if I were there," Peyton commented over the line.

"Yes, the pure muscle that is Peyton." Shay chuckled. "Anyway, we're gonna to need to hear these guys, so we're gonna remove our receivers now. Okay, Peyton?"

"If you're sure."

"We can't be distracted. Talk to you after we grab the coffin." Shay pulled her earbud out.

Lily did the same. "What are we going to do with a golden coffin? Isn't that kind of obvious?"

"After we grab it, we drive to a private airstrip. The Professor's sending some guys who'll take it back. We'll head to London so we can take a supersonic back. Easy shit."

The teen laughed. "But I wanted to see you try and take a golden coffin through Customs. The looks on their faces alone would be worth it."

"That kind of thing is easier than you think." Shay winked.

"Bringing strange coffins through airports?"

Shay shrugged. "Yep. Or strange artifacts. I smuggle a lot of things because it's too risky to get noticed by other tomb raiders and that sort of thing, but I'm not as worried about some Customs agent. It's the weapons, more than the strange artifacts, that are the problem."

Their cargo-loading preparations complete, Shay eyed the thirteen rocks.

Too bad that magic didn't last but the damned soldiers stayed around.

Shay drew her sword. "From here on out, don't speak or make noise if you can avoid it. I don't know when the army will show up, but my guess we won't have much time after we open the crypt."

Lily nodded.

The tomb raider took a few careful steps past the rune stones.

The sound of metal scraping against wood filled the air.

Shay narrowed her eyes and looked at Lily, who shook her head and shrugged.

The same sound came again, this time from a different direction.

"They're drawing swords," Shay whispered, tightening her grip on the hilt of her *tachi*.

Lily lifted her father's artifact and bit her lip, but her panicked expression made it clear it wasn't working.

She didn't use it last time we went on a mission. Wonder if she was trying to see if she didn't need to rely on it? Just like I worried about relying on James. Doesn't matter, though. Seems like it's not working.

I gambled and lost. Not her fault.

"Stay close," Shay whispered.

Lily nodded.

A light wind kicked up. The tomb raider's head swiveled back and forth. She looked for any signs of depressions in the grass and dirt, but there was nothing.

Completely fucking invisible. Sure. Yeah. Perfect.

Shay took a deep breath and slowly let it out. She could do this. She'd fought people in the dark when she was a killer. The only difference was that it was broad daylight, and she still couldn't see them. A little unnerving, but the principles remained the same.

Clear my mind and listen.

More draws followed, some closer than others. Adding in the original sounds, Shay counted forty enemies.

Forty invisible ghost soldiers. Yeah. This is fun. Very fun. Clear my mind. Clear my mind.

A soft moan reached her ears from her left.

Shay spun and slashed with the *tachi*. The sword slammed into something. A bright blue flash outlined a man's form before he collapsed into a pile of white ash.

Okay, thirty-nine to go. Hurray, me.

Shay listened for more moans and the scuff of boots. She spun to her right, and the ring of metal on metal sounded even though her sword appeared to have hit nothing but air. She hissed and pulled back slashing low then up.

Another ghostly soldier appeared, only to dissolve into white ash.

Thirty-eight.

The wind blowing behind Shay sounded slightly off. She spun, shoved Lily out of the way, and raised her sword just in time to block the blow from an invisible blade.

Lily scrambled behind Shay as the tomb raider stepped back and slashed to her side at the scuff of boots. Her blade separated the spectral form's head from his body before he dissolved into white ash that was blown away by the wind.

Thirty-seven.

The wind carried the sound of several more swords being drawn.

Well, shit. Maybe if I threw some dust? No, the ash is blowing straight into the wind. There's nothing I'm going to be able to do to make them visible. Clear my mind and listen. I can do this.

Shay spun toward a hiss, bringing her sword up just in time to knock a hidden blade away from her heart. She gritted her teeth as the sword sliced through her shirt sleeve, cutting her bicep. Ignoring her wound, she stabbed straight forward and made another pile of ash.

Her arm throbbed, and blood welled up from the wound.

Okay, he nicked me, but we're down to thirty-six.

Shay shifted the sword to one hand and made three quick throws with her adamantine knives. Three blue flashes highlighted the cursed soldiers before they joined their comrades as ash. The knives fell to the ground but looked unharmed.

Both her hands returned to the hilt of her sword.

Thirty-three.

The next couple minutes passed without Shay getting cut again, but she finished off only three more enemies. Her wound continued to throb, sapping her concentration.

Fuck. It's not like I've not been stabbed or sliced before. Don't know why this shit hurts so much.

Shay again spun and shoved Lily out of the way to block an attack. The whistle of a blade to her left brought her sword up, and she parried a second attack. The enemy was starting to gang up on her. The tomb raider would probably never know whether that was a sign of intelligence or was just an inevitable part of the spell that had bound the men to the area.

"Nine o'clock, one yard," Lily whispered.

Shay didn't even think before she thrust that way. Her blade met another soldier, and he drifted in the wind as ash. The girl's power had finally kicked in.

"One at ten and another at twelve, both half a yard." Lily stepped beside Shay to point and reinforce the location of the enemy.

Knowing exactly where the enemy was helped. Despite their numbers, the spectral soldiers lacked the swordsmanship they possessed in life. It was likely the only reason Shay hadn't been killed.

Lily kept her father's artifact in hand as she continued to shout directions and point. Shay's *tachi* reduced enemy after enemy to ash.

Twenty-five. Twenty. Ten. Five.

Shay panted, her arm on fire. She needed to close the

wound, but she couldn't spare the seconds to take a healing potion.

Lily stayed close to Shay. "Four surrounding you, evenly spaced out, with one directly in front."

The tomb raider rushed forward, slashing low. She didn't wait for her enemy to turn into ash before spinning and slashing to her left and right. More piles of ash appeared.

Lily pointed toward the last of the four. Shay sprinted forward and stabbed, but this time her blade met invisible metal. She twirled her blade around the hidden weapon until she found the body of the spectral soldier.

Just one more.

"He's right in front of me," Lily squeaked.

Shay twisted and shoved the girl out of the way. The tomb raider shot her sword up. Sparks flew as her blade scraped against the invisible sword of her final enemy. The soldier pushed down, and Shay hissed, the ache in her arm intensified by the force.

Two quick slashes and a thrust finished the final enemy. White ash now coated the entire area. It looked like it had snowed.

Shay sheathed her blade and winced. "Damn. They only got one hit on me, but it hurts like hell. Go get the first aid kit. We'll do a little analgesic spray, and I'll slap a bandage on it, then we'll get the coffin. A little cut isn't worth a healing potion."

The tomb raider shook her arm.

Beating forty invisible men. Not bad for a woman with a sword and a Gray Elf.

Hours later, Shay's eyes fluttered open. Her stomach tightened, and a few seconds passed before she remembered where she was. Safe. Well, safe enough. She was on a commercial supersonic flight back to Los Angeles.

Her arm throbbed and burned. She spared a glance at Lily. The teen slept peacefully in her first-class seat.

Shay rose and made her way to the lavatory. She'd thought the bandage and spray would have been enough. The wound hadn't looked deep enough to need stitches.

She closed the door and pulled up her shirt sleeve. She hissed from surprise rather than pain when she stared at the mirror. Her arm was swollen.

Shay removed the bandage. The clean slice before now was a pus-filled green, red, and black mess, like some nasty infection from a wound in jungle water.

With a deep sigh, she pulled a healing potion from inside her jacket pocket and downed the contents. Thirty seconds passed without any relief. Then a minute. Then two minutes.

It didn't work. What the fuck? How did it not work?

Shay held up the small blue glass potion bottle. What kind of wound couldn't be fixed by a healing potion?

16

As Shay stepped into Prophecy Affiliates, her entire arm throbbed and a fiery ache shot up it. She'd done her best to conceal the wound from Lily before dropping her off at the tunnels, but she knew the girl was suspicious.

The tomb raider didn't need Lily worrying about her or feeling guilty because her power hadn't been reliable. Shay had known the risks when she'd chosen to take on a dangerous tomb raid and bring along a tomb-raider trainee with questionable magic.

Sometimes your luck just runs out.

Madge looked up from the tiny magazine she was reading.

What the hell? They make pixie-sized magazines? I can barely find human-sized physical magazines anymore.

The pixie fluttered out her seat and sniffed a few times. "Something smells off and nasty. Did you not shower today?"

Shay rolled up her sleeve. "A healing potion didn't

work, so I'm guessing this is magical. I was hoping Tubal-Cain might know something or someone who could help."

Madge paled and made a face. "Damn spectrals. You're in luck. He's just in the back room. I'll go get him."

The pixie fluttered toward the back door. She lifted her hand, and the door opened without her touching it. She flew in, and about thirty seconds later, Tubal-Cain and Madge both emerged.

The pixie flew back to her chair and magazine, but the gnome walked toward Shay, clucking his tongue and shaking his head.

Not like I planned this. Cut me a little slack.

Shay shuffled toward a chair and dropped down with a hiss.

"Impressive." Tubal-Cain tilted his head back and forth. "And what, Miz Carson, were you doing to get this kind of wound?"

"Making sure Michael Galbraith didn't get brought back to life and making a shitload of money."

The gnome's brow lifted. "He was a very annoying wizard. And, what? One of his minions did this to you? That would be odd, considering the nature of the wound. It's definitely some sort of curse, but it feels much more like a spectral curse than a dark wizard's curse. Wrong smell, too."

Shay wondered how the pixie and gnome could just smell the thing and understand so much.

Magic is so fucking weird.

The tomb raider shook her head. "Not a curse. I had to grab a golden resurrection coffin. It was guarded by this invisible army of soldiers. One of them got a hit on me with his sword."

Tubal-Cain nodded. "Ah, I see. That explains it all. The festering of your wound is a result of the curse on those soldiers. I've heard of them. Not the poor bastards' fault... entirely. They messed with the wrong people centuries ago, and ended up, as a result, as the victims of very nasty magic that split their existence between different planes. Very rare thing, actually. Impressive in a disturbing sort of way."

Shay blew out a breath. If anything, her arm hurt more since she'd stepped into the shop. "Can't afford an excess of sympathy for anyone swinging a sword at my head. Those assholes were trying to kill me."

"Yes, swinging and almost landing a clean blow." The gnome chuckled. "You fought forty invisible spectrals without dying right then and there. I have to say I'm impressed, Miz Carson. You do have a knack for survival."

"I had a magic sword. It helped." Shay didn't feel the need to explain that Lily had also helped. She assumed that the gnome knew somehow, but there was no reason to give him the satisfaction.

"Don't be so modest, Miz Carson. Even with a magic blade, most single warriors would have been felled by such an army." He rubbed his chin. "I wonder if your blade was enough to truly destroy them, or if they'll return. It's an interesting thing to consider."

"Don't know. Don't care." Shay took a few deep breaths. "I got the coffin, and it's in good, safe hands and well away from any dark wizard cultists. My question for you is if you can do anything about my arm, or if I need to go to the hospital and fucking have them amputate it. It hurts like a motherfucker."

Tubal-Cain rolled his eyes. "It's just a little curse, no reason to be so dramatic. I have just the thing. You'd be surprised how often I see this sort of thing."

Shay let out a sigh of relief. "Good. How much do I owe you?"

"A favor. I'll even say a minor one." The gnome gave her an almost feral grin. "Or you could go and get it amputated. That would stop the pain and spread of the infection. It might be interesting to see how you deal with such adversity."

Shay forced a smile on her face. "I've grown rather attached to my arm. You have a deal."

Tubal-Cain clapped. "Excellent. One moment. I'll be right back."

He disappeared into the back and reappeared a minute later with a plain-looking black cloth.

The gnome offered the cloth to Shay. "Put it on the wound and wait. It'll only take a minute, but it'll be excruciating, so prepare yourself."

Shay shrugged. "Better than chopping my arm off." She grabbed the cloth and draped it over the infected cut.

Nothing happened for about five seconds, then the cloth suddenly tightened around her wound. She hissed. Tendrils detached from the material and threaded deep into her arm.

Shay closed her eyes and gritted her teeth. The ache became an inferno of agony. She managed to make it twenty seconds before she screamed, the pain knocking any other thought out of her head.

Then it stopped.

The tomb raider sat, hunched over, sweat all over her face, and panting. No burning, no pain, and no discomfort remained. She yanked the cloth from her arm. There was no wound or scar or even blood. The cloth fluttered to the ground.

Shay sat up. "Well, that was about as fun as crawling naked through glass."

Tubal-Cain grinned and shrugged. "I do try and keep things interesting."

When Shay stepped out of her Fiat into Warehouse Three, a sweet scent reached her nose. She tilted her head and sniffed a few times, trying to place it.

Peyton stood in front of a table near the oven kneading dough and whistling to himself. Flour covered the table, his apron, the floor, and even a wall yards away

How the hell did he manage that? Does he throw flour grenades in here?

Shay walked toward him, sniffing a few more times. Whatever Peyton was making, it wasn't pizza.

Peyton looked up from his dough. "Hey, Shay."

She searched around for a moment, spotting even more flour on walls, and a trail of floury cat footprints that led into the office.

"What are you doing?" Shay asked.

"Making cronuts. It's like a croissant and a donut had a baby."

"I know what they are." Shay snorted and rolled her

eyes. "I used to live in New York. That's where they were invented."

She blinked, realizing that several crates across the room were coated with flour. Some of the physics involved didn't seem possible.

Okay, I don't want to know. I'll just ignore it and hope he has it cleaned up by the next time I come.

Shay spun on her heel and marched back toward her car.

"Where you going?" Peyton called.

"I've got research to do."

Failure was the fire in the crucible of greatness. Every time a woman made a mistake, she should just think back, examine it, and figure out how to avoid making that mistake again.

Shay wanted to believe that, but her heart wouldn't let her.

No. Mistakes burned in her soul, reminders of her failure and the fact that she wasn't the best in the world at something. The best in the world wouldn't have screwed up and failed to recover an artifact twice.

At least in Antarctica she'd had the excuse of being outclassed by Yulia, but her first real failure as a tomb raider hadn't involved any witches, or even any enemies. Austria. Lake Toplitz.

Shay settled into a chair in front of a Warehouse Four table and set a book in front of her, *The Lost Treasures of the Third Reich.*

She'd gone for gold and a magical persuasion pin. She'd escaped with her life and diamonds. At the time she'd convinced itself it had been a good trade, but any tomb raid that ended without the artifact in hand couldn't be excused as anything other than a pathetic failure.

What? I think I'm okay to go back at some point because that trapped-log maze collapsed? What if some super-powerful water witch goes over and just parts the lake like she's Moses?

The job hadn't been finished. Even if she didn't care about the gold, she needed to go back someday and get that pin for her own sanity.

I don't fail. I only retreat temporarily.

Shay grinned. She'd make her mistakes part of her way going forward. The students might like to hear about Lake Toplitz. She wouldn't tell them, of course, about how she'd gone there to acquire the pin, but it'd be a nice entry point into the magical aspects of the Nazi regime and how their dangerous artifacts were now spread all over the world.

The tomb raider opened the book to Chapter Four, *The Lost Gold of the Third Reich*, and smiled.

Past failures might burn, but there was only one direction to go: forward.

"I'm doing pretty damned well so far," Shay mumbled.

17

Shay yawned and stretched her hands over her head as she stared at her bedroom computer. She missed James. He'd headed out of town for some stupid barbeque thing the same day she'd returned from England. They just kept missing each other lately.

She chuckled. *Guess this is what it means to be a busy couple with independent careers.*

The tomb raider tapped away, delving into the nastier and seedier corners of the dark web. Although Peyton's assistance had freed up her time so she could concentrate on artifact recovery, she didn't want to get too lazy and forget how to find information herself.

Peyton wasn't a piece of equipment, but a man. He couldn't guarantee he'd be with her forever, either by choice or tragedy. To that end, it was good to spend time during the week checking into her old online haunts for information and figure out what was new and hot in the world of murder and assassination.

Her phone rang with a call from Peyton.

"Huh, he's up late." Shay picked up the phone. "What's up? Trouble?"

"His heart didn't grow three sizes that night," Peyton answered. Panic was evident in his voice.

"What are you talking? Whose heart?"

He sighed. "My brother. I was just following up on Randy, and I found some people poking around looking for me, and I've traced them back to you. He hasn't given up completely. Like I said, his heart didn't grow three sizes. He's never going to give up."

"We did the *Christmas Carol*, not *The Grinch Who Stole Christmas*." Shay adjusted the phone so she could hold it with her neck.

She started tapping at her own computer. She wanted to verify what Peyton was telling her and make sure he hadn't imagined things in a fit of paranoia. After all, she'd spent months trying to instill paranoia in him.

"Same difference," Peyton replied. "The point is, he's still coming. He's just hired guys who are a little more careful and subtle this time. What are we going to do? Shit, shit, shit."

"The way I see it, you've got two options here." Shay frowned at a window that popped up. Peyton was right. His brother was still poking around.

You stupid dumbass. You're really trying to push me into killing you, aren't you?

"What are the options?"

"Option one: I become Old Shay and handle him in a very final and bloody manner. I can do it in such a way that it won't be linked back to you, which is easy anyway because you're officially dead, even if the authorities are still poking around."

Peyton groaned. "I…I don't think I can do that."

"You wouldn't have to do it, and he tried to do it to you." Shay clicked back to her previous screen. "I would do it. A threat to you is ultimately a threat to me. Even though the cartel is gone, it's still in my best interests for the assholes of the world to think Killer Shay is dead."

"But he's my *brother*, Shay."

Shay snorted. "Are you fucking kidding me? The guy paid to have you killed. This isn't like you two had a falling out during Thanksgiving dinner over which candidate you supported in the last election. The fucker wanted you dead because even though he was already rich, he was a greedy son of a bitch who wanted even more money he didn't have to earn. If it were me, I would have gone and stabbed his ass already."

"Well, I'm not you, *or* him," Peyton snapped. "All right?"

Shay pulled the phone away for a minute, surprised at the man's vehemence, even if she wasn't surprised at his reticence. "Yeah, you aren't, which is why I mentioned a second option. This one doesn't involve shooting, stabbing, or blowing Randy up."

"And what's that?"

"Your brother isn't some sort of super-resourceful badass, and he doesn't have any magic. His power comes from one thing: money."

"Yeah, so? What's your point?"

Shay chuckled. "Come on, Peyton. In this day and age, money is mostly just bits on a computer. We make his money go away. It's not like you're ever going to need it, and your other relatives have separate accounts. I doubt they're going to loan him piles of money so he can chase down the ghost of his dead brother. From what I can see, he's not talking to anyone else anymore."

Peyton sighed. "Yeah, when I looked into it, that's what I saw, too. Without my dad as the glue, the family died when I did."

"Then we should do it. Hey, Lily and I presented a dark future of poverty. Scrooge had his fucking chance to reform, now the future's gonna come barreling down at him. He should have listened to Marley."

"I guess."

Shay snorted. "It's either that or I kill him. Understand?" She inserted an extra edge into her voice. "This is a loose end we need to tie up, one way or another, and I can't continue looking the other way."

"I'll start tracking down all the necessary account information," Peyton murmured. "I'll set it all up for a single script. A decapitation strike."

"Good. We don't need to do this right away. If anything, we want to take him off-guard. Observe and report. Got it?"

"Got it."

Shay took a deep breath and slowly let it out. "I know this shit is hard, but it's also necessary. Not for me, but for you."

"I know. Talk to you later." Peyton hung up.

I should have fucking killed Randy for real right after I fake-killed Peyton.

Shay shrugged. She felt no pity for a man who brought on trouble himself.

The tomb raider returned to her dark web searches, once again more interested in the future than the past.

A few minutes later, her eyes widened at an entry on a hitman forum.

"Son of a bitch." Shay groaned and stood. She had someone she needed to talk to, but first, a quick trip to Warehouse Five was in order.

Shay marched up the street in the middle of the night with her hands in her pockets. She hoped that when she ran into her targets, they'd be reasonable. The whole point of this little trip was intelligence-gathering, not ass-kicking, even if that would be fun.

I could have killed all you assholes the last time we tangled.

Someone shouted something in Cantonese from an alley, and several men laughed.

Shay sighed and turned the corner to confront a half-dozen men from the 25K Triad. They stood around smoking foul-smelling cigarettes.

She recognized each from the previous encounter, and more than a few still bore bruises from that last meeting.

The man she'd tagged as their leader pushed off from the wall. She'd later identified him as Johnny Lee.

"Oh, fuck," Johnny uttered. He scrubbed a hand over his face. "This is bullshit. Total bullshit."

The men exchanged nervous glances. A few swallowed and slowly inched their hands toward their guns.

Shay gave them a thin smile. "Let me make one thing really fucking clear. I didn't kill any of you last time because I was trying to keep the peace, but if any of you go for a gun, I will end you right here. Also keep in mind, last time I managed all that shit without even using my gun, so do you really want to see what I can do in a shoot-out?"

Johnny lifted his arm to stop his men. "Okay, fine. What the fuck is this about?"

"I need some info from you."

He laughed. "Are you for real?"

The other men just stared at her like she'd lost her mind.

Shay nodded. "Oh, I'm real. A real nightmare if you piss me off, but I'm also fair."

Johnny narrowed his eyes. "Fair?"

"You guys are businessmen, right? Criminal businessmen, but still businessmen, and a businessman should never do something for free. I'm not here to ask for a favor. I'm here to pay for a service."

The gangster stood up straighter and adjusted his jacket. "Yeah, that's true. We were only after that one bitch because she stole from us, but you paid us back. We can appreciate that."

"I'm gonna reach into my pocket and pull something out. Don't do anything stupid, and keep in mind if I'd wanted to gun your asses down, I would have already done it."

Johnny nodded to Shay, then his men.

The tomb raider pulled out a small music box. "This is a minor artifact. Can play any song you think of. Just hold it and think. I figure it's a fair trade. You give me info, and I give you the artifact."

"Why us?"

"Because little suspicious birdies have told me you are in contact with the Phoenix Gang."

Johnny tensed. "Yeah, we know them. Not saying we're friends or enemies. Just that we know them."

Shay tossed the music box toward the gangster, and he snatched it out of the air. He stared at it for a moment, and a few seconds later it chimed out what sounded like a sad attempt at a hip-hop melody sans bass line. The gangster's face brightened.

Johnny looked up from the music box as it continued its melodic hip-hop demonstration. "What do you need from the Phoenix Gang?"

"I haven't heard of them before in LA, and they're interested in James Brownstone. That makes me interested in them."

All the men winced, and Johnny looked down. "I don't know if we want to get involved in this shit, not if it involves Brownstone. We don't need him thinking we're with the Phoenix Gang and grinding us into dust like he did the Harriken."

Shay snorted. "If you don't want him thinking that, you should help me. From what I hear, these Phoenix assholes put a hit out on him, and I want to know where they came from."

Johnny took a deep breath and slowly let it out. The music box ground to a halt.

"They're not new," the gangster muttered.

"Huh? I haven't heard of them before."

He looked up. "They aren't new. I'm not lying. The Phoenix Gang? They're guys from different LA gangs that Brownstone wasted in the past, but they'll take anyone as long as they go through an initiation and swear they'll help with the death of James Brownstone. The leader used to be in the Harriken. Low-level asshole. He wasn't in town when the Granite Ghost finished them off. Some are from street gangs, a few Harriken, a couple of friends of bounties. Shit like that."

Shay blinked. "So this whole gang is just some big-ass Brownstone Hate Club?"

"Yeah." Johnny shrugged. "Look, those fuckers came to us and wanted us to bring in 25K guns and men to help them with Brownstone. We told them to fuck off, that we wanted shit to do with poking Brownstone. Everyone with half a brain knows what happens to fuckers who mess with Brownstone."

"Who's the leader?" Shay demanded.

"This big asshole who goes by the name Tsuchigumo."

"And where does he hang out?"

Johnny shrugged. "Don't know. They are very tight-lipped about that shit."

Shay snorted. The gangster had named himself after spider-like demons from Japanese myth, and given what she'd run into during her time in the country, they probably weren't myth.

This asshole, though, is just some arrogant fuck, and I'm so going to end him.

"Okay, thanks. Your prize is that nice artifact and the fact I'm letting you walk out of here. I suggest you avoid being around the Phoenix Gang for the next few days. I have a feeling they're about to suffer some lethal accidents."

Shay sprinted forward, and the gangsters all scrambled backward with panic on their faces. The tomb raider didn't attack them but instead ran and jumped, grabbing a low-hanging ladder on the side of the building. She leapt from the ladder to a ledge, then pushed off toward another ledge.

She quickly scaled the building and disappeared into the night. The slack-jawed gangsters stared up in wonder.

———

18

Shay took a few deep breaths as she loaded spare mags into her tactical harness. A quick call to Peyton had confirmed he was at Warehouse Two, not Warehouse Three, which would make concealing what she was about to do much easier. As far as he knew, Shay was following up on a few minor tasks for Tubal-Cain.

I told James the old Shay was dead, but here I am getting a bunch of weapons to go fuck up an entire gang.

She gritted her teeth. Killing someone in self-defense during a tomb raid was one thing, but she planned to track down men with the express purpose of murdering them.

Shay slammed a magazine into her 9mm and slipped it into a holster. She double-checked her adamantine knives, then several backup knives.

She reached up to check her auburn wig. The wig and contacts, along with a little putty to change her face, would be enough to keep people guessing. The triad members would obviously understand what the hell was going on, but they didn't even know her name, and they were afraid of her and James already. After she killed the Phoenix Gang, they'd be even more scared.

James could probably handle the Phoenix Gang. After all, he'd destroyed a good chunk of the Harriken even when she wasn't helping him. But his solution to dealing with an enemy group was to lay waste to everyone in sight, and it had a way of escalating until the situation was a clusterfuck.

Should I tell him? Does he have a right to know? The hit's on him, not me, and here I am planning to go handle it without even letting James know.

Shay moved to a tray of grenades: sonic, fragmentation, and incendiary. She grabbed several frag grenades. Unlike with the triad, her plan didn't involve survivors.

The problem with incendiary grenades was that their fires could spread to other buildings. She didn't need to make trouble for non-gang members.

If the Phoenix Gang weren't immediately stopped, everything would spiral out of control, just as it had with the Harriken. Sure, James could win against normal gangsters, but what would he do if a magical assassin showed up? The Collector had almost killed them both in Japan.

For that matter, if James didn't know they were coming, he might not have a chance. His amulet protected him, but it wasn't like he slept with the thing on. The man had already had his house blown up.

Shay picked up a submachine gun and inspected it before slinging it over her shoulder. Her 9mm pistol might not be enough.

Maybe an RPG if I have to knock on someone's door the hard way?

The ex-killer-turned-tomb-raider took several deep breaths. Sometimes loving another person meant cleaning up problems they didn't even know they had.

When she was out of the country and someone had used magic to pretend to be her, James had handled the problem.

I was annoyed when he tried to get Peyton to not tell me about the AET wanting me, but that was half his fault since I was helping him.

Shay sighed. If she handled the problem herself, there was no point in even telling him. There was no reason for James to worry about something in the past.

She picked up an RPG and blew out a breath. "Okay, Tsuchigumo, you've gotten the wrong woman's attention."

The thug smashed into the bottles behind the bar with a loud crash, several breaking open and spilling their contents all over the man and the floor. The man groaned and climbed to his feet.

Shay sneered. "I'd feel worse, but you're the owner, and you're a piece of shit."

She hopped over the bar and slammed her fist into the man's face. He flew backward and smacked against the bar, then moaned and slumped to the ground.

The man tried to go for a gun, but Shay smacked it out of his hand and had her 9mm pointed at his head a second later.

The temporarily-reborn killer narrowed her eyes. "I'm in a really shitty mood. You're the fourth guy I've had to talk to today, and people keep trying to do what you did, which is feed me bullshit when I've got a really fucking simple question. Where the fuck does the Phoenix Gang hang out?"

The thug shook his head and spit blood at her feet. "I don't even know who the fuck you are. Why should I help you out?"

Shay laughed. "Of course, you don't know who the fuck I am. I'm new in town, but I've got business with the crew of washed-up losers." She pointed her gun at his crotch. "Or I can leave you half a man."

He winced and raised his hands. "Okay, okay. I'll tell you. They've got this place in Florence. It's a massage parlor that's a front for whoring. The Happy Ending."

Shay rolled her eyes. "Seriously?"

The thug shrugged. "I don't work for them. They've just come by here a few times. They throw around money. Good tippers, you know?"

She kept her gun up as she advanced on the downed man. "Just remember I was here. The only reason I smacked you around was because you made it hard for me to get the information I want. The Phoenix Gang is done today. If I track them down, and I find out that they knew I was coming, then I'll know you told them, and I'll be forced to come back here and finish what I started."

The man threw his hands in front of him. "Woah. Woah. Shit, calm down, chick. I ain't telling them nothing. I don't know how they done you wrong, but I figure if someone brings on that kind of heat, they've got that shit coming.

"If I were those fuckers, I would have left town anyway. They're all stupid shits who were lucky to survive Brownstone. And forming that gang? That's like surviving a hurricane and then building your house even farther out on the beach."

Shay lifted her gun and hopped the bar. "If Brownstone's a hurricane, then I'm a tornado. I hope their fucking insurance is paid up."

Shay parked her van in an alley a couple of blocks down from the massage parlor. Given the location, she couldn't open up with an RPG or another heavy explosive without attracting too much police attention, not to mention the risk of killing women who were just trying to make their way in the world.

No. She was there to kill the members of the Phoenix Gang; no more, no less. Part of being an expert killer was not being sloppy.

She took a deep breath. To her surprise, her heart rate hadn't increased. There was something almost comforting and familiar about what she was about to do, in a way it hadn't been when she and James had gone after the cartel.

Killing someone when it's not self-defense just feels like a job.

Shay slipped on dark sunglasses. Between her wig, contacts, the glasses, and the putty, none of the witnesses stood a chance of identifying her in a line-up. The only thing she needed to do was make sure there were no electronic recordings that could be harvested for facial recognition algorithms.

She hopped out of the van and tapped the silver bracelet on her wrist. The clock was ticking now that she had a broad-spectrum jammer activated. Her long dark unseasonable coat concealed her tactical harness and belt and still had a stylish flair, unlike the awful gray monstrosities James liked to wear.

The killer made her way toward the massage parlor and pulled a short-range EMP device out of her pocket as she approached the back door. It emitted a loud buzz when she pressed the button, and a quick glance to the side confirmed that nearby traffic lights and street lights were dead. Yet another thing starting a timer.

It didn't matter. Shay would finish and escape long before any cops showed up. It wasn't like their response times in this part of town were all that fast. She continued up the street. A few people glanced her way but didn't pay her much notice. They probably thought she was a prostitute.

She walked into an alley behind the massage parlor. A huge gorilla in an ill-fitting suit and four layers of gold chains around his neck looked at her.

"Who the fuck are you?" the man barked. He took a drag off his cigarette.

Shay sighed. "I was looking for the Phoenix Gang."

"And why the fuck are you doing that?"

"I heard there were looking for girls. You know, working girls."

A grin split the man's face and he dropped his cigarette to the ground, stubbing it out with his toe. "Oh, that shit's different." He looked her up and down with a frown. "I can't see nothing with your glasses and that coat. Come over here and show me what you've got. Don't want to waste anyone's time."

"You with the Phoenix Gang?"

The gorilla nodded. "Yeah."

"I heard the Phoenix Gang are made up of people who used to be in other gangs."

He chuckled. "Why do you care, bitch?" He marched over to her. "I wasn't in a gang. I worked security for this sweet-ass arms dealer. That shit was the easiest money ever, but then that fucker with the messed-up face, Brownstone, ruined it all. Put me in the hospital and sent my boss to prison."

Shay stuck out her lip and reached inside her jacket. "Sounds tough."

"Yeah. It was, but now I got a new crew." He licked his lips. "And it comes with fringe benefits."

Shay's knife was in his throat in a flash. He tried to speak, but only a gurgle and blood came out. She yanked her knife back and kicked him to the ground, the dark alley hiding his body.

She wiped the knife on his suit and sheathed it before pulling out her 9mm and throwing open the back door.

Red emergency lighting provided eerie illumination inside the building. A backup generator, probably. It saved her the trouble of using a wrist light or the light atop her SMG.

"Yo, Phil," someone called from a nearby hallway. "Where the fuck are you? You were supposed to be done smoking fifteen minutes ago, you lazy fuck."

Another suited thug stepped into the hallway. Shay put a bullet in his head before he could even register what he was thinking. The gun's report echoed in the hallway.

She'd thought about bringing the magical silencer she'd acquired recently and going room to room, but had decided against it. She wanted the Phoenix Gang to be spooked and know someone was here to kill them.

Several other doors opened, and a few scantily dressed women peeked out.

"If you're a woman, get the fuck out," Shay yelled.

The women darted the other way, some screaming.

Shay kept her gun up, waiting for men to emerge from the rooms. A confused-looking older man emerged from one of the rooms with his pants around his ankles.

"Is she coming back? I already paid!"

Shay narrowed her eyes and waved her guns. "Get the fuck out, asshole."

He hiked up his pants and hurried after the women.

A few other men emerged and rushed the opposite way once they saw Shay's guns. All of them looked like disgruntled or frightened customers.

Two suited goons wearing chains rounded the corner. Shay's gun spat death, and both men went down. She kicked in each door to ensure they were empty. She could barely make out the blood splatter at the end of the hall in the low red emergency lighting.

Shay stopped where the hallway turned and listened. Her experience in England reminded her of the importance of relying on her other senses.

"The bitches said it's some chick," someone whispered.

"A chick? Fuck, you think it's the mother of that one bitch? She said she'd come for us."

"Nah, them bitches probably just got spooked. It's probably those triad assholes or the Demon Generals. We'll show them. We just wait here until they turn the corner, and we'll fucking fill them with lead."

Shay grabbed a grenade, pulled the pin, and tossed it.

"What the fuck? Grenade!"

The men managed to scream just before the grenade exploded. Shay turned the corner and frowned. One of them was still alive. She pulled a knife and slit his throat before continuing through the blasted and blood-splattered abattoir that had once been a hallway with three men in it.

Shay holstered her 9mm and reached under her jacket to pull out the submachine gun. She readied the weapon and continued down the hallway, her heart rate steady. No fear. No concern. Just cold-blooded delivery of death.

The hallway led to another hallway with office doors on each side.

Everyone innocent is long gone. This should make shit easy.

Another thug barreled out of one of the doors and squeezed off a round. The bullet zipped by Shay's head. She put a burst into his chest, and he fell with a yell.

You almost had me there, asshole, but you have to hit me on the first try.

She readied another grenade and tossed it at an angle into the open room. Two men dashed out a second later, only to fall to the hail of bullets from her SMG.

At the next room, Shay didn't even bother to open the door. She held the trigger down and sprayed bullets from her gun until it clicked empty. A quick mag ejection and reload later, she kicked open the door to find two dead gangsters.

You don't win battles of attrition by hiding, assholes.

She snorted. They were a gang made up of survivors of defeated gangs. Maybe these were all the men who knew when to run and hide. If that were true, they should have run from LA and hidden as far away as possible.

The hallway ended in a wide lounge, complete with a full bar. The long shadows and red light gave the room a sinister atmosphere. Several tables had been overturned.

Shay didn't enter. Instead, she stood a few feet back in the hallway and listened. There was heavy breathing and hurried murmurs inside.

She ducked and threw a grenade behind a patch of overturned tables. Men leapt and ran away, shouting. Others popped up from behind the bar, the muzzle flashes of their pistols and shotguns cutting through the crimson darkness.

Shay rushed to the side, spitting bullets out as her grenades exploded. Glass shards, drywall, and wood exploded around her. A bullet slammed into her leg, and she dropped with a hiss.

Gotta finish me, assholes.

She leapt for a table, continuing to hold the trigger down and nailing several of the gang members. Bullets perforated the top and middle of the table, and she took a moment to send her last grenade over it.

Should have brought a flash-bang or two. That's the problem with not purposely killing people all the time. You get rusty.

Shay ripped a healing potion from her pouch and

downed it. She had one more, but so far the Phoenix Gang had mostly proven they were good at dying. No wonder they'd placed a hit on James instead of going after him themselves.

A second later when the grenade exploded, she took advantage of the chaos and rolled behind another table. Her leg had already started to heal.

Shay repaid the shouts of a charging man with a shot between the eyes. She nailed another man through the table, then ducked behind the bar.

Several soft moans, but no more hurried whispering. Shay counted, then popped up, aiming down at the bar. The two surprised gangsters trying to hide there didn't even get their guns up before she finished them.

The front doors exploded in a shower of glass as four men with assault rifles opened fire. Shay rushed to the side of the room in a zig-zag motion, returning fire. Blood blossomed from the chests of the men as they fell to the ground.

A Japanese man in a finely-tailored suit stepped around the corner, the glass of the shattered door crunching underneath his polished shoes. Unlike almost every other gangster she'd run into he sported no chains, and he wore a scabbard with a *wakizashi*. The man was obviously ex-Harriken.

The man pulled up a sleeve to reveal a glowing spider tattoo.

"Am I supposed to be impressed?" Shay asked.

"Do you know who I am?" The man rested his hand on the hilt of his sword. It almost made Shay wish she'd brought the *tachi*. There would have been some poetry in killing a former Harriken with the enchanted Japanese sword.

"Tsuchigumo, the leader of this pack of trash." Shay ejected her mag and reloaded. He obviously wasn't going to try to shoot her for whatever reason. "You're obviously ex-Harriken."

He smiled, but it didn't reach his eyes. "You're very powerful. I could use you."

"You don't care that I just slaughtered your men? Kind of an asshole, aren't you?"

"The weak perish. The strong survive. Such is nature. Such is civilization. The Harriken were weak, and now they are gone." Tsuchigumo shrugged. "I would ask why you've done what you've done, though."

"Because you assholes can't learn a lesson. All your little bullet sponges are here because Brownstone fucked up their gangs, so what do you do? You try to pick a fight with him again by putting a hit out on him." Shay shook her head. "I don't get it. If the strong survive, why hate on Brownstone?"

"Only a fool leaves a sword pointed at his heart. Brownstone must die for that reason alone."

Two other gangsters stepped around the corner behind their leader. One carried a sword and looked Japanese. Shay assumed he was another ex-Harriken. The other was a huge white man with chains. She couldn't begin to guess what pissant gang or group he came from.

Both held guns but kept them pointed down. Unlike their leader, barely-contained panic infected their faces as they surveyed the scene before them: mangled corpses and dying men, walls, floors, and ceiling painted with blood.

Shay kept her attention on the men in front of her, near-complete calm settling over her and her heart beating steadily. She was doing what she needed to do to protect her man.

She lifted her gun. "It didn't have to be this way. All you had to do was leave well enough alone."

"Leave this bitch to me," Tsuchigumo ordered. He drew his sword.

Shay sighed and lowered her SMG to her side.

"You recognize the futility of fighting me?"

"I'm guessing your little glowing tattoo is some sort of protective magic." Shay reached into her jacket and pulled out an adamantine knife. She pulled back her arm. The knives weren't the best for throwing, but they were balanced well enough.

"You think a knife will work when a gun does—"

Tsuchigumo tumbled to the ground, the knife sticking through his eye.

Shay snapped up her SMG and put a round into the gun arms of the remaining two men. They collapsed to their knees, grimacing in pain. She stepped slowly toward them, stopping to lean over and yank her knife out of the dead leader's eye. She wiped the blood off on his jacket before sheathing it.

"Oh, fuck," one of the survivors cried. "Oh, fuck. Oh, fuck."

One deliberate step followed another. The crunch of the glass marking her every step as she approached the men, her gun at the ready.

"Do you know why you're not dead yet?" Shay asked, her voice a near-monotone.

The men both shook their heads.

"Because I need you to answer a few questions. First question, assholes, I'm guessing there are more men in your little gang?"

They both nodded.

"About twenty more guys," the second survivor offered. He gritted his teeth, obviously in pain from his gunshot wound.

"Then I guess I need the two of you alive to spread the word, because someone needs to know what happened here. Congrats. I know James Brownstone likes to send messages, so go tell the world what happened here. Learn the fucking lesson the Harriken and so many other gangs didn't learn. If you fuck with Brownstone, you die." Shay leaned forward and offered the men a cold grin. "If you even look at him the wrong way, you die. The only reason anyone is dead today is that you assholes thought you could put a new hit out on Brownstone. You understand?"

The men both nodded. She lifted her gun, and the second one covered his face before wetting himself.

Pathetic. These assholes thought they had what it takes to take down James?

"Get up," Shay barked. "And get the fuck out of here. If you know what's good for you, you and the rest of the gang will pack up and run as far from LA as your little legs will carry you, because next time I have to show up—or *he* has to—every last one of you fuckers dies."

The men both managed to stand. Their wounds dripped blood on the floor as they turned and ran out of the building.

Shay let out a long sigh. Sirens sounded in the distance. Time to go.

She shrugged, her heart still as calm as if she were watching the Weather Channel. It had to be done. She would always protect her man's peace.

19

The next day, Shay tapped on the keyboard in the Warehouse Two office, her thoughts returning to the slaughter the night before. Guilt was far from her mind. If anything, despite the calmness during the slaughter, the old excitement from a well-executed killing job threatened to bubble up.

I'm not surprised. I was a killer because I was good at it. Even if I can distance myself from what I did and not enjoy it for the sake of the killing, that part of me is still there, even if I told James the old Shay was dead after we killed the cartel.

Was this really so different, just because I killed people who weren't a direct threat to me? I'm so full of shit.

Peyton knocked lightly on the door. "Everything okay?"

Shay looked up, blinking. "Why wouldn't it be?"

"You're just...really quiet this morning. Way more than usual. It reminds me of the old days right after you first killed me."

"The old days?" She snorted. "Whatever. Shut the fuck up."

Peyton swallowed once and took a deep breath. "I was poking around, and there's chatter on the dark web about how someone slaughtered a new gang in town last night, the Phoenix Gang. About three-quarters of the gang got killed at a massage parlor they were running."

"And why the fuck do I care about that? Gangs can all go cut each other's dicks off for all I care. Less scum to worry about."

"Just...you know. It's not exactly like you helping and/or killing a large number of criminals is unprecedented in recent history, between you helping with the Harriken, assassins, and the Nuevo Gulf Cartel. And the last one wasn't all that long ago." Peyton shrugged. "From what you told me before, the whole cartel thing was supposed to be kind of turning point. Shay 2.0 and all that. You weren't out taking care of business, were you? Taking out a few more people for old time's sake?"

Shay gave him a death glare. Some things Peyton didn't need to know, for both their sakes. He needed to stop pushing.

He withered under her attention. "Never mind. Sorry I asked. I just forgot for a minute that I was riding the scorpion across the river."

"Never forget people's true natures," Shay muttered. "You'll live longer that way." She turned back to the computer.

"Um, there was actually something else I needed to talk to you about." Peyton winced as Shay snapped her head back his way. "It's work stuff, not personal."

"What?" Shay barked.

"Just a weird message I got through one of your contact emails. Someone wants to meet with you, Miss Professor." Peyton frowned. "You *are* still a tomb raider, right?"

Shay gave him another death glare.

Peyton threw up a hand. "Okay, okay. No need for that kind of look, just checking. Anyway, the thing is, the guy who wants to meet with you? It's not about a tomb raiding job."

"Then why do I give a shit?"

"I would have told him to go away, but he claimed it was government-related and sent some confirmation codes that seem to support that, like high-level top-secret-clearance shit." Peyton shrugged. "And with all this Project Nephilim and Project Ragnarok stuff, and after what you found out about..."

"James?"

Peyton nodded. "Yeah. Well, the thing is, it's extra-weird because the guy's specifically asking to meet with Professor Carson, not Aletheia."

"Huh?" Shay frowned. "What are you talking about?"

"Oh, crap. Sorry, I wasn't clear. You know I'm filtering most stuff for you these days, but yeah, it's a request to meet with the professor, not the tomb raider. Nothing in his message suggests he even knows about your tomb raiding activities."

Shay frowned. "That's weird. Maybe it's a trap. Just because he's acting like he doesn't know doesn't mean it's true."

"It could be, but I don't know. It'd be a better plan to

lure you out to the middle of nowhere overseas and kill you if that is what he wanted." Peyton shrugged.

The tomb raider sighed. "Guess I need to go see who this is and what he wants. Where does he want to meet?"

"At a diner in Huntington Park."

Shay nodded slowly. "Well, guess we'll see what he has to say."

A quick inspection of the outer perimeter of the diner revealed no hidden enemies or suspicious vehicles. The level of drone traffic wasn't unusual for this part of town.

Shay stepped into the diner with a frown on her face. A dark-haired man in silver glasses and a navy-blue suit waved from a corner table, his back against the wall. Defensive seating.

Yeah, look at you, Mr. Careful. At least you're not a total amateur.

She frowned, her hand reaching into her purse and settling on the comforting grip of her gun as she walked over to the man.

"You're the one who wanted to meet me?" she asked.

"Yes, Professor Carson." He gestured to a seat across from him. "Please join me. We have a few things to discuss."

Shay noticed a small mirrored cube not larger than a die sitting on the table. "What's that?" She pointed at it.

"A nice little trinket that lets a man have a private conversation in public. Listen carefully, and you'll see what I mean."

She frowned and sat. After a few seconds, she realized she couldn't hear any background noise.

"Neat trick. Magical or technological?"

The man laughed. "Now where's the fun in telling you that? The real fun is that when people look, our mouths movements will be randomized, so if they're good at reading lips, they'll understand that something's wrong."

"Who the hell are you?" Shay slowly pulled her hand out of her purse. This was all too elaborate for a simple assassination.

"Daniel Goldstein, and I work for the CIA." He shrugged.

Shay laughed. "Seriously?"

He nodded with a wry smile. "Seriously."

"I assume that's not your real name."

He shrugged. "For now, it is. Names in my line of business are very fluid. Were you born with that name?"

Shay ignored the question. "What does the CIA want with me? I'm not a spy."

Daniel shook his head. "This isn't about counter-espionage, at least not in the sense you're thinking."

"And what do you mean by that?"

"I've read some of your lectures, both your UCLA stuff and your previous stuff. You're an expert on revised history, and you have a keen mind that sees through a lot of bullshit."

Shay eyed the mirror cube. "Like what kind of bullshit?"

"Like the fact that everyone now believes that if you look at weirdness in history, you have to assume it's Oricerans."

Her stomach tightened. "And you don't agree?"

"Let's just say that I've seen enough to convince me that Oricerans aren't the only aliens who like to mess around with Earth. Most want to stick their heads in the sand and pretend that's not true because it just becomes scary for them after they thought they figured it all out."

Okay, so this guy's got a good head on him and is careful.

Shay nodded. "Uh-huh. What kind of things have you seen?"

Daniel flashed her a smile. "I need to keep a few cards close to the chest until I know I can trust you. I know you're probably not used to that kind of thing as a professor, but in my world, trusting people can easily lead to death."

Okay, Peyton. I have to give you major credit. You gave me a fake identity deep enough to fool a guy from the CIA.

Shay leaned forward. She couldn't deny that she was interested. "Okay, so what does this all have to do with me?"

"The short version is that I'm putting together my own little team within the CIA using both Company and external resources. I'm concerned that not everyone in the government has the best strategy for dealing with potential extraterrestrial threats, and a lot of them are more interested in suppressing things rather than getting out in front of it. I need to help push this in a different direction." He gestured toward her. "I'm impressed with you, and I think you've got potential as a researcher. It'd be nice if you had more skills, but the research skills are useful enough."

You asshole. I've faced down invisible armies and rusalka. I've found vimana keys. Have you done that? I've probably faced more weird shit than half the CIA combined.

Shay kept a smile plastered on her face. "Oh, I'm not exactly useless outside of the classroom. Digs in remote areas aren't always the safest thing, you know."

Daniel looked her up and down, but the look in his eyes was clinical and detached, with not a hint of a leer. "Guess you keep fit for all that field work, and you're right. The world's not a safe place, and it's become even more unpredictable these last few years."

"Yeah, something like that, and what about you?" Shay glanced over her shoulder, having just noticed no waitress had ever stopped by. For all she knew, the entire diner was a CIA front.

Daniel gave her another too-perfect smile. "What *about* me?"

"You've got your little silence cube, which suggests you aren't just a pencil pusher." She almost mentioned the defensive seating but didn't want to tip him off that she was more than a professor.

Daniel laughed. "I get out into the field for fun on occasion, sure."

There was an ease to the man she found disarming, but there was also an almost forced quality to it. Every once in a while, the façade would drop for a second and the eyes of a calculating and dangerous man looked at her.

What's your deal, Goldstein? You planning to track down aliens and kill them to make sure they don't threaten the country? If so, I better keep close to you to protect James.

Shay made a show of glancing at her phone. "I'm flattered by all this, but I do have to go. I have a lecture to deliver at the university."

Daniel raised an eyebrow. "A CIA agent shows up to

recruit you to help him with, among other things, investigating aliens, and you're concerned about being late for your day job?"

The tomb raider shrugged.

He laughed. "I know I'm making the right choice in reaching out to you. You must love your work."

"I do."

"Okay, then. I'll see you around, Professor Carson. It should go without saying, but just to be clear, I'd rather you not mention our little conversation to anyone." A hint of menace crept into his eyes. "And remember, I *am* with the CIA."

Shay snickered and stood. "Who would believe me even if I told them?"

"Good point. Until next time, then."

She offered him a final polite nod and turned to leave, still unsure whether to trust the man or if he knew more about her than he was saying. She wanted to believe Peyton had fooled the CIA, but the whole conversation also could easily be some sort of long-play manipulation by the government.

Does he work for Project Nephilim or Ragnarok? Maybe they figured out I'm on to them.

Shay stepped out of the diner with doubts swirling in her mind.

20

Shay threw her arms out to her side to get the attention of the students filling the room. The lecture on Lake Toplitz was going even better than she'd anticipated.

They are eating this shit up. Nice.

"Deadly traps. That's what I'm talking about. Of course, even with all that gold most likely sitting on the bottom of the lake, no one's been able to recover it, and there have been fatalities.

"Given what we know about magic now, we can't dismiss out of hand that magical traps haven't been set up to guard the treasure. Even though magic was contained before the truth about Oriceran came out, that's not the same thing as saying there was no magic. So, many of these lost treasures have to be considered much more dangerous than before."

Murmurs swept the room as Shay advanced her presentation slide from a picture of gold bars to an image of an eagle pin.

"And the gold's not the end of it," Shay continued. "Which argues for traps even more. We now have a fairly good idea that the Nazis had access to a number of magical items, and many of their great treasure hordes likely also included such things."

Shay aimed her laser pointer at the picture of the eagle pin as she finished her lecture, the students all listening with rapt attention.

"Recent evidence suggests that artifacts like this might be on-site, and at least one might have been an artifact of magical nature—an enchanted eagle pin. Unfortunately, any useful artifacts are lying under piles of unstable logs at the bottom of a deep lake. It's not exactly an easy site for recovery, and any sane archaeologist would stay well away from it because of the dangers."

"What about the gold?" someone shouted from the back. "Is it all still there, you think?"

The rest of the students laughed.

Shay shrugged. "We can only presume that most, if not all, of the gold is still there, along with the pin and other artifacts, if it was indeed at that location, which it very well might not have been." She shook a finger. "Now, I know some of you are thinking this is just a lot of legend and second-hand rumor, but when you examine the strands of evidence together and how they point at one another, you quickly see that they all point the same direction."

She pressed a button on her pointer/clicker, and a picture of Heinrich Schliemann replaced the eagle pin. "In these sorts of situations one can't ever be sure, but remember, everyone thought Schliemann was a nutjob until he found Troy. Sometimes, you're just going to have to be fine with being called crazy until you prove you're right."

The students laughed again.

Mary, who was sitting in the front, shot her hand up. "Professor Carson, I just wanted to say you really did your research. It's like you were there."

A few other students nodded in agreement.

Basing a lecture around an actual tomb raid might have been risky, but with the artifact secure under all the logs, Shay wasn't worried that anyone was going to retrieve it anytime soon.

Shay shrugged. "That's the power of using primary sources." She glanced up at the clock. "And it looks like it's time to go. Thank you all for coming."

She spotted a familiar man in a navy-blue suit in the corner.

Came to check up on me, huh, Goldstein?

Shay waited at the lectern for a few minutes, fielding a few final questions as the students filed out. Once the last student had left, Daniel made his way toward her lectern and set his silence cube atop it.

"Interesting lecture," Daniel offered.

"I try to make it engaging. It's hard enough to get students to care about the past, and sometimes harder to get them to care about the changing views of the past."

The CIA agent smiled. "It really does sound like you were there. You sure you haven't been?"

Shay laughed. "I've been to Austria, won't deny that, but it's not like I'm the kind of person who'd go diving for sunken treasure. I like to keep things safe and academic."

"Sure. Maybe." Daniel stared at her.

Does he know?

"What?" Shay asked.

"What if you *could* be the kind of person who could go diving for sunken treasure, or at least help supervising it, but you wouldn't be at risk?"

Shay frowned. "What the he... What are you talking about?"

It was easy to maintain her Professor Carson mask in front of the students, but the CIA man set her on edge, and the real Shay burned to come out and challenge him in voice and manner.

"Among other responsibilities, I need to recover the pin you discussed in your lecture. I'm well aware that it's a magical persuasion pin."

Shay watched the man, looking for some sign of discomfort or nervousness, but he displayed the same overly-pleasant demeanor he'd shown during their earlier discussion.

"That pin is dangerous." Shay shrugged. "It might be better off at the bottom of that lake where no one can ever abuse it."

"Oh, I know it's dangerous, which is why it shouldn't stay there. Twenty years ago, big deal. It'd take a lot of tech and time. But these days, with all these abracadabra, you never know when someone might march in and get it. Serious artifacts can't be left around for random elves or wizards to pick up." Daniel pointed at Shay. "And that's where you come in."

"Oh?"

"I want you to act as the supervisor for a team I'm putting together to find the gold and the pin in Lake

Toplitz. If you agree, you'll get ten percent of the value of the gold."

Shay almost laughed, again wondering if Daniel knew she was a tomb raider. "That's a lot of money for a project supervisor."

"Well, consider it a fee to exploit your knowledge of the area and your experience concerning this lake. I won't be on site, but I'll make it clear that everyone is to follow your orders. You won't have any trouble leveraging your knowledge."

Shay shook her head. "I'm interested in the job, but I want to make it clear that I haven't been to Lake Toplitz."

"If that's how you want to play it, fine." Daniel shrugged. "We all have our secrets, Professor Carson."

Shay sighed. "That said, I know how dangerous the area is. If I'm going to be involved, I want ninety percent."

Daniel wasn't polite enough to turn away. He laughed straight in her face.

He wiped a mirthful tear away. "Come on, you work for a university. You should know the government doesn't pay that much."

Shay shrugged. "Not my problem. Enjoy the magically booby-trapped log maze. It's your problem now. Just being around there might get me blown up."

The CIA agent smirked and scratched his eyelid. "I can convince them to give you thirty percent, which is really damned generous. You'd never have to work again if you didn't want to. No more lectures to spoiled kids."

"Like I already told you, I like my job. There's only one other thing I need before I agree to take the job."

"What's that?"

Shay pointed at him. "The truth about why, if this is your responsibility, you won't be coming along on the jo…expedition."

Daniel chuckled. "Aren't you the curious one?"

"Most academics are. That's why they choose that path."

Daniel watched her for a few seconds before nodding. "I've got another artifact that has priority, and I can't go to Austria to play right now."

"What's the other artifact?"

He shook his head. "Let's just say that's need-to-know. Right now, you're not part of my team. You're a contractor. Maybe we can revisit that after this Austrian job, if you're willing to take it."

Shay nodded. "Okay, I'll supervise your team, but that doesn't mean I'm committing to anything else."

Daniel smiled. "Of course. Congratulations, Professor Carson, you're moving up in the world." He grabbed his cube and stuffed in his pocket.

Shay said nothing else as the man walked toward an exit.

What the hell am I doing cozying up to some government agent? If this guy digs enough he'll eventually figure out the truth, but I do need to make sure he's not sniffing around James.

She frowned. If Daniel already knew the truth, then everything might be some sort of big test. The CIA wasn't renowned for their ethics. He might know all about her current career and past and not give a damn.

Shay sighed and ran her hands through her hair. What with Peyton's brother, James' alien secrets, helping Lily, and now subcontracting for the CIA, her life had gotten damned busy.

21

Shay frowned as she stepped on the escalator. The flight to Salzburg had gone well enough, and her team had already arrived. It should have been a simple matter of meeting her contact and being driven to Lake Toplitz.

Of course, shit was already going south.

She feigned checking her phone while using the camera to check behind her. Three men. She'd spotted them watching her the second she'd stepped off the flight. They were almost comically obvious with their oh-so-painful casual clothes that didn't match their buzzcuts and practiced movements, and did little to hide suspicious weapons bulges from a person who knew what to look for.

A person like Shay.

Who are these assholes?

The tomb raider who was pretending to be nothing more than a simple professor made her way through the crowds and away from the rental-car pick-up area. If something went down, she didn't need people witnessing her ass-kicking skills and Austrian cops taking her in for questioning.

Shay continued walking away from the main gates. The crowds thinned out, and the men picked up their pace. She no longer had any doubts that they were following her.

She glanced around, looking for cameras. The great thing about airports was they often wanted the surveillance to be obvious, with the thought that it would be a deterrent in and of itself. The cameras were sparse in the area, so as long as she controlled where she walked, she could easily avoid them.

The tomb raider altered her course with that in mind. After a quick final survey of the area, she turned the corner and entered a long, empty hallway.

This will do. Probably don't have much time before someone shows up.

Shay stepped a few yards into the hallway and waited, reaching into a hidden pocket in her jacket. About thirty seconds later, the three buzzcuts walked around the corner. They blinked, clearly surprised to see Shay waiting for them.

She didn't hesitate, just charged the men. A quick throat-punch sent one man to the floor, and an elbow to the second's face put him down. She whipped out a butterfly knife from the hidden pocket and had it to the third man's throat in an instant.

"Who the hell are you?" Shay demanded.

"Fuck you, bitch," the man responded. His accent sounded vaguely French.

Could he work for Durand? No, this doesn't seem like his style.

Shay slammed a fist into the man's stomach. Two more quick punches had him on the floor unconscious. She strolled to the two other groaning men and knocked them out with kicks to the head.

Shit. Someone's either targeting me or the expedition. Shay took a picture of the men, then glanced both ways.

She couldn't kill them without causing too much trouble. At least, she couldn't kill them *there*, but she was sure she would be seeing them again soon.

It was time to contact Peyton and get a few things figured out.

Her rental Mercedes barreled down B145. She'd called ahead, and the team was expecting her and already almost set up. The only problem was that she doubted they'd be ready to do anything before nightfall, and that was even before considering her new friends from the airport.

Shay's phone rang with a call from Peyton, and she answered it on speakerphone.

"Find anything?" she asked.

"Those guys are trouble."

Shay snorted. "I already knew that. Can you be more specific?"

"Turns out they used to work for Alpha Explorers. "

The tomb raider frowned. "So, what, this is revenge for Oak Island?"

"I don't think so." The clicks of Peyton's typing came over the line. "I don't honestly think they know who you are. I mean, that you're a tomb raider."

Shay glanced into her rearview mirror to make sure she wasn't being followed. "What do you mean?"

"The new guys they work for aren't tomb raiders in the same way Alpha Explorers were. Instead, their new strategy is to track research around the world. They find out who the leader is, capture them, get the info, kill the leader, and steal the prize."

"Perfect. Fucking idiots. If they know enough to target me, then they know enough to come after the expedition."

"Probably. You could tell everyone that someone's after you."

"No. I don't want my new CIA friend getting suspicious and digging deeper. It's a miracle he hasn't seen through the fake identity shit, especially the college stuff."

Peyton huffed. "Hey, that was quality work."

"Not saying it wasn't, just saying this guy's CIA." Shay frowned. "I'll just have to take these assholes down, along with any friends, without anyone seeing me do it."

Peyton laughed. "Good luck with that. Sounds impossible."

She snorted. "You forget what I used to be."

"Nope. Not that. Never that. Don't think I'll ever forget again."

A soft wind blew over the surface of Lake Toplitz and cooled Shay's face. Some of the tents ruffled in the wind. This wasn't a tomb raid. It was a true expedition.

So this is what it feels like.

She grinned at the dozen men working on finishing

their inspection and unloading of three huge submersible cargo drones from trucks. The drones all had manipulator arms, and with careful guidance, would be able to help move the logs and ferry out the heavy gold.

The tomb raider wasn't sure if they'd be able to gain access to the magical artifacts without an actual person. It depended a lot on the nature of the spells, although her last trip to the lake might have already triggered all the defensive magic.

A girl can hope.

The first time, she'd come to the lake by herself and nearly died. Now she had an entire government-sponsored expedition. It was nice to be appreciated for her knowledge rather than her killing skills.

Is this what could have been? Do I have my own Ghosts of Christmas Past, Present, and Future hanging over me?

Shay wanted to be free of her past but had mercilessly gunned down, stabbed, and blown up the Phoenix Gang the other day. She'd never escape it if she kept running into its bloody embrace whenever it was convenient.

She sighed.

Wonder if I should tell James about working for the CIA as a consultant?

Shay frowned and shook her head. Daniel knew too much about aliens, which meant she needed to make sure he was kept far away from James. Too many plates were spinning. At some point, they would start to fall, and Shay would have to make some hard choices about which ones to save.

The beautiful orange-pink of the setting sun and the deepening shadows announced the coming darkness. The team had erected light poles along the edge of the lake and behind their fenced perimeter, but she didn't like the idea of wasting time poking around at night, especially if they ended up deciding to send divers.

"Just finish getting everything ready," Shay shouted. "We'll hit the lake at dawn with the drones and figure out possible dives after that. If we're lucky, maybe we won't have to dive at all."

One of the team members, an engineer named Bill, rushed over to her. "The drones are almost ready to go, but we're having some trouble with the interface. There's a lot of interference. Your report didn't say anything about broad EM frequency interference up here. Do you think that's a side effect of the magical defenses?"

Shay frowned.

You guys don't see the obvious, do you?

Daniel had secured the necessary permissions from the Austrian government and provided her with a skilled team of engineers and divers, not to mention all the best equipment, but it was painfully obvious that these people were not tomb raiders.

Even though they weren't aware of the incident at the airport, they should have been more suspicious.

It wasn't as if they didn't have any guns. Everyone possessed at least some proficiency with a firearm, and they had a weapons locker in one of the cavernous green tents. Unfortunately, shooting a gun and having the paranoid instincts honed by tombs raids were separate things.

The reality was that if they had been tomb raiders they would have realized the immediate implications of the interference, and that it wasn't some spell messing with their equipment.

Someone's jamming us. If they're jamming us, they're going to be coming at us soon.

The surrounding pines and other trees grew thickly enough to hide a small army.

Shay sucked in a breath. She could tell everyone to arm up, and they could try and repel an attack, but the men's lack of tactical experience would make an already-chaotic situation disastrous.

No, she needed to handle this problem herself.

Shit. As far as Daniel's concerned I'm Professor Shay Carson, a slightly eccentric academic. I'm lucky he hasn't seen through my fake identity already. If I start killing people he'll figure out who I really am, and that won't end well for Peyton or me. It's not like I can take on the CIA.

Shay glanced at her tent. She'd brought a few of her toys, even if the expedition members and the CIA agent didn't know about them.

"Let's pack it in for the night," she announced. "I want everyone bright-eyed tomorrow morning. Maybe by then, the interference will have cleared." She clapped. "And I want us to find ourselves some gold."

The men laughed.

So the enemy is probably jamming us and watching us. The smart play would be to let us go to sleep, wait an hour or so, and then ambush us.

Shay retreated to her tent and pushed in, closing the flap behind her. She dug through several biometrically-sealed metal boxes until she found a small one with a DNA lock. She pressed her thumb to the plate and hissed at the familiar burn. The lock popped open, and she opened the lid.

Her three adamantine knives lay inside, nestled atop her folded tactical harness and a 9mm with a few magazines.

If they ask about this, I'll just claim the knives are valuable artifacts I dug up a long time ago, and I always want to make sure I can protect them.

Shay slipped on the harness and loaded a mag into the pistol before holstering it. She sheathed the knives, then slid under the open sleeping bag on her cot. Now it was time to wait.

Thirty minutes later, when chatter had drifted to silence and everyone was in their tents, Shay carefully and slowly unzipped the front of her tent and crept out into the darkness.

The lights had all been killed, and their only real defense was the pop-up chain-link fence they'd deployed. The intent wasn't to stop people, but rather the wildlife that might wander in.

Shay crept through the darkness, resisting a snicker. It wasn't even like she was doing anything wrong. Taking out the people who were trying to attack her and her team was simple self-defense, but she was skulking through the darkness like some scumbag criminal.

She just couldn't tip her hand to Daniel. It was too much of a risk to her and everyone she cared about.

This is why superheroes have secret identities, but am I a superhero or a supervillain?

The tomb raider smirked as she made her way to the fence and vaulted over it without trouble. A stray flash of green caught her eye.

Sloppy, assholes. Really, sloppy.

Shay rushed toward the forest, keeping low to the ground until she hit the tree line. She was grateful there wasn't a full moon. Some nearby branches crunched, the quiet sound almost a scream in the still night.

The shadowy forms of a half-dozen men emerged from the tree line. All wore night-vision goggles and held rifles.

These guys definitely mean business.

The tomb raider had already moved well to their side in an attempt to flank them, saving her from being spotted right away. She hurried until she was behind the men. The earlier fight at the airport must have convinced them that she wasn't a simple college professor, which would explain the jamming and night assault.

The men raised their rifles and opened fire, their muzzle flashes lighting up the night. The tomb raider sprinted behind them. She'd planned to do this quietly, but since they'd already fired, she might as well take the easy path.

Shay pulled out her 9mm and blasted toward each muzzle flash. Three men went down with screams. She rushed toward a nearby tree, and a counterattack by one of the men blasted bark into the air. She returned fire, downing another man.

The two surviving night raiders rushed toward Shay, one laying down suppression fire as the other tried to flank her. She put two quick rounds into the first man, but the final man flanked her just in time to exchange shots.

She hissed and fell to the ground as a bullet ripped through her forearm. Unfortunately for the other man, Shay's bullet blasted right through his night-vision goggles and into his head.

Shay took a deep breath and reached into a small pouch on the harness. Her last healing potion. She'd need to get more, but she had to finish the expedition first.

Hope this was the main group of assholes.

She downed the potion, the agony vanishing from her arm as her wound closed.

Shouts erupted from the expedition camp.

Shay holstered her weapon and sprinted toward it. She needed to reach it before they turned on the lights or she would have a lot of explaining to do.

The shadows of several of the men emerging from the tents appeared. Everyone's attention was focused on the source area for the gunfire and not on the tents. Shay vaulted the fence with ease and hurried into her tent.

"What's going on?" Shay shouted as several light poles clicked on.

"Gunfire."

Shay stuck her head outside the tent to look for damage from the gunfire. She didn't see anything obvious, so she grabbed a jacket to cover her harness and the bullet hole in her shirt. "Grab a couple of guns, and let's check it out."

Good. Now that the riffraff's clear, we can get what we need tomorrow.

Daniel arched a brow as he skimmed the incident report the next day. Extraction of the gold containers and other valuables was proceeding even faster than he'd anticipated. Professor Carson claimed she'd never been there before, but she seemed to have an uncanny understanding of where to find things and the magical defenses.

Hmm. She's hiding something, maybe some sort of clairvoyance artifact. That'd make a lot of sense, but that's not the real problem. Can't believe the expedition was attacked.

There must have been a leak. I was sloppy, and could have lost a good resource in Professor Carson.

He narrowed his eyes as he continued reading the report. Six men dead from gunshot wounds before the expedition team had even pulled their weapons out of the storage lockers.

That meant someone had taken out a well-trained team armed with assault rifles and night-vision goggles in the dark. One major question remained.

Who?

22

"No one else showed up?" Peyton asked over the phone.

Shay checked her GPS as her Mercedes continued down the road. She wasn't that far from Munich. "Nope. Did you find anything else on them?"

"Those six guys were the main group, so unless they've done a bunch of recruiting in the last few days, you shouldn't have anything to worry about. You get everything from the lake, then?"

"Yep. We did some additional sweeps to verify, and the team collected everything. I stayed with them as far as Salzburg, where some very serious and angry-looking individuals in suits showed up to take control of the cargo. The government payout will come to me in a few weeks."

Peyton laughed. "But you're used to getting paid right away."

"Shit, it's the government. I should be happy it doesn't take months." Shay changed lanes to let several cars zoom by. "Besides, I have this job you found me in Munich for an easy payout. Just have to raid a tomb that's a little more recent."

Peyton sighed. "Weird mix of people buried at Munich Waldfriedhof, everything from Nazis to Nobel Prize winners."

Shay laughed. "Well, I don't care unless they rise from the dead. Just gonna pop into the crypt, grab the diadem, and get the hell out. I'll hit the cemetery at night, so I don't have to worry about running into anyone."

"Well, running around a cemetery at night isn't my idea of fun, even if it is to get an artifact that lets you tell lies."

"Beats going under a lake or into rickety old tunnels underground that might collapse on you." Shay grinned. "Don't worry. I'm sure this will be an easy job."

Daniel sighed and shook his head as another man stepped out of the crypt with a briefcase in hand. The CIA agent had been afraid of this ever since he'd read a report the British government had hired Hollingsworth Retrieval Specialists to recover the diadem.

Maybe if he'd finished his previous job a few hours earlier he wouldn't be in this situation, but scoring a minor artifact after his previous mission would be a nice bonus. He'd been lucky to be able to get to Munich so quickly.

Between the lake, my last job, and this one, it's been a good week. I was right to bring on Carson to supervise the lake expedition. I might have missed out on the second artifact otherwise.

The Hollingsworth tomb raider continued walking away, oblivious that he was being watched.

Sorry, my friend, but I need this more than you do.

Daniel kept low, darting from gravestone to gravestone. The English tomb raider whistled a jaunty tune as he continued away from the crypt.

The CIA agent wasn't above killing when necessary, but Hollingsworth men weren't actual scumbags so he'd have to do this the hard way.

Daniel jumped up from behind a gravestone and the tomb raider spun toward him, his eyes wide, just in time to get a good old-fashioned American punch to the face. He lost his grip on the briefcase.

The tomb raider stumbled back with a grunt. "You're not a bloody zombie."

The CIA agent shrugged. "Not yet, anyway. Just walk away, and this doesn't have to go badly. I've got nothing against you, but I need that artifact."

The Englishman raised his fists. "Come on, you bloody arsehole. Let's see what you got."

The men exchanged a few quick jabs, but couldn't land a solid blow. The tomb raider charged low and tackled Daniel with a grunt. The men sprawled to the ground and rolled, slamming their fists into their enemy's body and head.

Daniel untangled himself and hopped back to his feet, then smashed one of his black wingtip into the tomb raider's stomach. The other man grimaced and stood, his face bloody and battered.

The Englishman shook out his hands. "You're tougher than you look, prick."

"Like I said, I've got nothing against you. I just really need that artifact."

The other man sneered. "And I really need you to kiss my arse."

"I..." A blur in the corner of Daniel's eye caught his attention. Had he miscalculated? Was there another man there?

He spun toward the movement just in time to spot a dark-haired woman in a jacket rushing away from the men, briefcase in hand.

"Damn it! Oh, for fuck's sake."

The men exchanged glances and sprinted after the thief.

Daniel picked up his pace, trying to close on the woman. There was something vaguely familiar about her. Maybe a tomb raider he'd read about in a file or someone from another country's intelligence agency? He'd solve the mystery when he caught her.

The woman leapt atop a gravestone and jumped from it toward another gravestone, then jumped again, sending her to the edge of the roof of a tall crypt. She grabbed the lip of the roof with one hand, pulling herself up, the suitcase still in her other hand.

The English tomb raider grimaced but continued running after the thief on the ground level as she jumped from rooftop to rooftop. "Now, that's just not bloody fair."

Daniel considered shooting her, but he didn't want to kill someone without at least seeing their face.

Another few quick vaults and jumps sent the woman over an internal cemetery fence.

Both men slowed to a jog. There was no way they'd catch up.

The Hollingsworth tomb raider looked at Daniel and shrugged. "And she wasn't yours?"

Daniel shook his head. "I take it she wasn't yours?"

The other man shrugged. "How did she move like that?"

"Artifact, I'm guessing." The CIA agent rubbed his sore jaw. "Well, we don't have a reason to fight anymore. Unless you're aching for it?"

"No point." The tomb raider stared after the vanishing form of the dark-haired woman. He shrugged and walked away. "Fuck, I just wish I knew where she gets all those wonderful toys."

"Maybe it's not an artifact. Maybe she's a Light Elf."

"Light Elf?" The tomb raider eyed Daniel. "Is that what you're going to tell whoever you're working with?"

Daniel shrugged. "Better than saying some nice lady ran off with the prize."

"How about those Drow? I've heard a lot of people blaming shit on them lately."

"Nope. A Drow would have killed us. It'd have to be a Light Elf."

The Hollingsworth man snorted. "Those damn Oricerans."

"Maybe not." Daniel furrowed his brow and tried to remember if he had seen a wand.

"Maybe not?"

"It could be a former Silver Griffin," Daniel suggested.

"Huh. A witch?"

Daniel's phone dinged, and he pulled it out. "Sorry. Have to take this." He gave a polite nod to the tomb raider and started walking away. No use wasting more time thinking about who the thief might be. He'd lost the artifact, and given the presence of a tomb raider, it wasn't shocking that someone else had shown up.

Need to be more careful.

He clicked on the alert message, and a satellite image appeared of the graveyard. One needed a good eye for imagery analysis, but his experience let him spot the hiding humanoid form atop a mausoleum roof. The time stamp showed it was only a few minutes ago. Apparently, this mysterious witch or elf was still in the graveyard.

Trying to wait us out, eh?

Daniel glanced over his shoulder to confirm that the other tomb raider was heading the opposite way before jogging toward the edge of the graveyard toward the building hiding the mysterious thief.

He reached into his jacket and pulled out a small sonic grenade as he closed on the building.

"Here goes nothing." The CIA agent tossed the grenade.

The dark-haired woman shot to her feet and tapped something on her ear. "Fuck." She turned and leapt, wincing as the grenade whined and blasted out its stunning frequencies. She tumbled over the edge of the fence. The briefcase flew out of her hand and landed on the other end of the fence, close to Daniel.

The woman stumbled away until she managed an unsteady jog.

Some sort of quick-neutralizing wave patterns? Nice tech. She's no amateur.

Daniel ignored her, instead heading over to the briefcase. He picked it up and opened it. The diadem lay inside.

He smiled. "Sorry, whoever you are, but I guess I get to

go home now after using one of my wonderful toys without any guilt."

About a half-mile from the cemetery, Shay slumped down in front of a tree, her head still throbbing.

"Shit. I can't believe I lost it. I don't even know how he tracked me down. I figured he would have been long gone in the opposite direction. Fuck. He's a lot better than I thought."

"But at least you didn't get caught," Peyton replied through her earbud. "And you're getting thirty percent of the lake haul, so it's been a good few days even without the diadem."

Shay rubbed her temples. "I just didn't expect to run into Daniel in Munich, of all places. Find anything on him yet?"

"I did my due diligence, and I couldn't find anything."

Shay snorted. "Not surprising. The guy is a government spy. Keep digging. I don't know what his deal is, but I want to know who he really is and what he's doing for the government."

"What do you mean? You don't think he's just a CIA guy interested in aliens?"

"I don't know whose side he's on." Shay blew out a breath. "And I can't begin to even think about trusting him until I do."

A day later, Daniel placed his hand on the palm scanner, then leaned forward for a retinal scan. He finished with a DNA scan from the surface of his thumb. The door beeped, and the lock popped open.

He stepped through with a smile aimed at the attractive middle-aged dark-skinned woman sitting behind the cherrywood desk and reading a tablet. She was wearing her usual white pantsuit.

"Hello, Miss Rose." He set the briefcase on her desk.

"Agent Goldstein." Her gaze cut to the briefcase. "This is it?"

"Yes, although I had some interesting company on my way to get it."

"So I heard." The woman gave him a thin smile. "But you handled it well enough."

"I always do." Daniel shrugged. "I've already logged in almost all the nice government-issued toys and weapons you let me borrow."

Miss Rose nodded. "I'm surprised you didn't use some of them on that little Munich trip."

"Oh, no reason to let some idiot from Hollingsworth see my coolest stuff." Daniel shrugged. "Sometimes the most efficient and low-tech way is the best."

The woman snorted. "Maybe if you'd used a toy, you wouldn't have had to chase down this other woman."

"Maybe, but it doesn't matter. I caught up with her in the end."

"I suppose." Miss Rose tapped the tablet. "You've not checked the Torino in yet, I see."

"Oh, I was going to do that next. It's hard to part from such a nice little piece of technology."

"And the modifications? How were they?"

Daniel smiled. "The armor was excellent, as were the aquatic modifications. The sensors were a nice touch. Maybe a tad overkill for the mission, but I can't complain too much. All in all, though, everything worked very well indeed."

Miss Rose set the tablet down. "I'll pass that on to R&D. I'm sure they'll be glad to hear it."

Daniel grinned. "A man can never complain when he gets to play with such nice toys."

23

S hay moved her arms back for support as she inverted herself from the hammock. Her muscles tensed but didn't burn as she held the position and stared at Bella, who tried the same movement only to slip into the hammock with a frown.

She'll probably be pissed if I laugh.

Kara and Janelle were still attempting a basic star inversion. They both managed to rest on their tailbones with their hands gripping the side of the hammock, but when they tried to let their bodies fall backward and opened their legs to stabilize their position, they kept falling.

Everyone needs better core strength. The running helps, but it's not enough.

Shay righted herself and moved into a star inversion, then bent her right knee and hooked her foot across the front of the hammock to hold the position. Every muscle in her body was worked by her normal routine, but a little aerial yoga was a nice change of pace.

Janelle settled her butt into her hammock and laughed at Shay. "Apparently, everything I've ever seen about archaeologists in movies is true." She winked. "They should call you Professor Buff instead of Professor Carson. You're like a freaking acrobat up here."

Kara sighed. "When you guys mentioned aerial yoga, I thought this had something to do with the *Little Mermaid*."

Everyone laughed, and Shay let the smile linger on her face.

It felt nice to be stretching and soaring in the air, free—almost as free as she felt when she was doing parkour. After her recent busy days of taking on gangsters, recovering lost treasures, and losing an artifact to a CIA agent, that freedom tasted all that much sweeter.

She also had a date with James that night, and *she* got to pick the restaurant.

Bella finally managed her star inversion. "You know what would make this even better?"

"Hot guys doing it too?" Kara suggested.

"No. Some wine."

Kara, Bella, and Janelle laughed.

Shay smirked.

This sort of calm freedom was why she needed these friends. They would never be told the truth about her life, but when she was with them, she didn't have to worry about anything but a good time. She could approach something that still felt so strange at times: relaxation.

"Maybe next time, girls," Shay suggested with a bright smile. "Maybe next time."

Shay paced across the front of the classroom and nodded toward a world map that had various outlined new continents, including Atlantis.

"As we've discussed today and during this lecture series, the key to revised history is not blindly accepting that every myth is an accurate representation of past history, but viewing such myths as a jumping-off point that can help lead you to the truth."

Shay clicked the presentation ahead to an elaborate oil painting of Rhazdon. The Atlantean's hair tendrils were more wild and serpentine than realistic, though it did look grand on the large screen.

"We went through the classic view of Atlantis earlier in the lecture and discussed the ramifications of there being a lost continent that was once populated by ancient and powerful beings who were beyond the other societies of their time."

The students nodded, many leaning forward with their attention focused on Shay.

The tomb raider glanced at the screen. "The important thing to keep in mind is that our legends humanized the Atlanteans, despite the fact we know now that they were a very non-human race and had access to powerful and dark magic." She advanced to a slide marking Atlantean energy transfer monuments all over the world. "The existing myth clearly has many holes, such as suggesting primitive humans could have repelled the Atlanteans militarily. It's obvious now that was a later addition to the myth. It was added to establish some agency for the oppressed human cultures that had to deal with Atlantis while still passing along the story of the ultimately magic-related sinking of the continent. The truth was in front of us the entire time, even if it had been covered by a few coats of paint."

Several students laughed, and a few eager students, including Mary, scribbled a few more notes.

"The other thing to keep in mind is that although Atlantis is one of the more impressive lost continents, it's likely not the only land mass lost either to time or magical manipulation. We're just now beginning to understand how much of even our geological history has been misrepresented either because of misunderstandings or magical manipulation.

"So, I'll stress what I've stressed before. Continue to question and continue to push for the truth. Don't assume that what I've told you in these lectures is the truth, so much as the best I can offer given what we now know." Shay smiled. "Any questions?"

Mary's hand shot up.

Still not sure if I find her annoying or refreshing, but at least she never asks dumb questions.

"Yes, Mary?"

"You mentioned how they discussed a metal called orichalcum in the legends, and that there's still debate about whether it was platinum or some other alloy, maybe even magical. Have any of the ancient metals been established to have been real?"

Shay chuckled and couldn't resist drawing from her other life. "Adamantine, long thought fictional, is a real if very, *very* rare metal, but as to whether orichalcum is real, I don't honestly know. Historians and archaeologists are still heavily debating that." She clicked the presentation slides back to a picture of some coins. "Some of the traits associated with the metal suggest something magical in nature, and we might interpret ancient authors' reports of it being mined out as a reflection of a lack of access to sources on Oriceran or some sort of Atlantean metallurgy magic that modified existing ores." She sighed. "Right now, the problem is that we still have a lot of gaps in this history, but academics continue to reach out to Oriceran scholars in an attempt to learn more about the fine details of the Atlantean culture from a day-to-day perspective."

Another student raised his hand.

"Yes?"

When the student asked if Poseidon had been real and an Atlantean, Shay couldn't help but smile. They might be naïve kids who didn't know about the darkness in the world, but perhaps they were better for it. They might be able to see truths that her blood-shrouded eyes would never spot.

Shay almost wanted to laugh. Over ten years as a killer, and she'd never thought she'd find something that gave her the same satisfaction.

I don't know who the fuck I am anymore, and for once that doesn't scare me.

Later that day, Shay loomed over Peyton's shoulder in the office.

"Okay, you've had time to think about it, and time to set things up," Shay commented. "We have both confirmed Randy is still looking for you. Even if he's trying to be more subtle, he's still there. It's time for this scorpion to ask you a very simple question: Should I give in to my nature? The offer is still on the table."

Peyton slowly shook his head. "It's like I told you before... I just can't bring myself to let that happen, even with everything he's done."

Shay nodded. "That means the only thing left is to divest him of his fortune. Even if he goes begging to your other relatives, he'll be in a bad position."

Peyton scrubbed a hand over his face. "Which means he'll hunt twice as hard."

"Randy's not a hacker. All he can do is hire them, and without a lot of money, he won't be able to." Shay shrugged. "And I'm hoping he'll finally take the fucking hint and give up."

"And if he doesn't?"

Shay's expression darkened. "Then he'll meet me again, long before he finds you, and the only ghost will be him a few seconds later."

Peyton gave a grim nod and turned back to his keyboard. "Sorry, Randy. I really didn't want it to go down this way." He hit Enter and activated the script. "You tried to kill me, brother, so I'm doing the next best thing to you."

FINIS

The countdown begins till the move into the new house! Appraisal next week and an actual closing date, at last…

Plans are already afoot for big gatherings like a weekly Sunday dinner. When I lived in Chicago in a tiny apartment my kitchen was always full of people. If someone wanted something out of the stove, everyone on that side had to get up first. For the first time in my life, I will have an actual dining room. Okay, empty at first but not for long.

A fellow author already lives in my new subdivision and has the lowdown on gatherings. A friend emailed me with info about nearby yoga classes that are donation-based, and another group has started monthly dinners at different restaurants near my new home.

That's what happens when we get bold enough to step out and make a change when things are okay but could be better. Doors fly open.

I like bold moves. I like writing my female lead characters as bold women who you would want as a friend and you know if there was trouble, they'd be running ahead of you to check it out. Bold moves take an internal operating system that doesn't ask, what can I lose, but instead is forever curious about what could be *gained*.

A system that operates off trust that in the end things work out.

That's how Michael Anderle and I work together, mixed with some swearing and a very healthy sense of humor. The swearing is just for fun too and I'd like to say it's Anderle but if you've read The Leira Chronicles you know that would make me a fucking liar.

Things don't go the way we want to all the time – covers are late, or a blurb needs to be rewritten or the wrong book is sent out. But, we look at what we can do to fix things, come up with solutions that put our readers first, ask for help from the right sources... and keep moving.

Doesn't slow us down from looking for the next bold move and seeing how we can reach out to fans more, write more good books and just keep going. Even when we spend money on things that don't pay off, we sort through it, take away some lessons, adjust, shake it off and see how we can optimize what we did do.

The results speak for themselves. We have some of the BEST FANS out there and the ranks are growing and we're having a blast in the Facebook Fan Groups sharing our lives and giving away prizes and answering goofy polls, plus chatting about all those books.

Back to the topic of the new house. By hanging out with Anderle for the past couple of years, I've gotten even bolder. You can't stay on the Anderle rocket ship if you aren't prepared to just buckle up and go! When this house showed up on my radar, even though I gulped at its size, I went for it.

But that's not the top of the mountain for me. I have no idea what that will be until the day I take my last breath. My goal is to spend the rest of my days building my tribe, reaching more fans with more good books, enjoying the hell out of that house, and having a lot of fun. I suppose an ever-expanding amount of that will be my mountain top. More adventures to follow.

First, THANK YOU so much for reading our book, and our *Author Notes*!

Three years ago, my wife was working and getting ready to go to ESCRS (a European Society of Cataract and Refractive Surgeons), which happens in the beginning of September every year. During those (about) ten days, I would pull out of the digital drawer a story I had started one year before and finish it.

That book would be published on November 2, 2015 as *Death Becomes Her*. Less than three years later, the series and the company that book helped usher in would affect thousands of people and thousands of authors because of the opportunities it would herald in the Indie Publishing community.

One of those opportunities became a relationship (for me) with Martha Carr.

I met her in Austin, TX after an event where I spoke in front of about eighty people. Many of them were already authors and many were writers. Few of them (I think) believed they could take what I said and implement the changes in their publishing career.

Except Martha.

If there was ONE person who had the justification for telling me to go screw myself, that I didn't know anything, it was Martha.

She had already been published by Traditional Publishers (the big companies) and had a column that was sent to hundreds of newspapers across the nation over a career spanning thirty years.

I was just an author that was selling some fiction for the last nine months.

For some reason, she believed I wasn't bullshitting anyone, and chose to come up and speak with me afterward. That conversation began a professional (snort) relationship where one year and one month after our first book came out, she steps into her new home, which was made possible by her efforts with LMBPN.

And believing that crazy author Michael Anderle.

I've had a blast working in Oriceran with Martha Carr. We have laughed together, (practically) cried at times, and cursed together and at each other, but one thing Martha has NEVER done is lose faith in me.

For that, I will forever be grateful.

I don't have a problem believing that I am a professional author. What I lack is belief that I'm anyone special who helps others' dreams come true.

Martha is slowly helping me understand that I am.

So, thank you, Martha. I appreciate the many times you say "thank you" and "you ass" (often in the same sentence, but I digress.) You have supported our efforts with an upbeat attitude when shit was hitting the fan so many times. And you are still here, and we are still making fans happy.

May your book *Peabrain* reach #1 in the Store, and I have to say "you beat me, you ass" one time in our careers ;-)

(But, you know, only once. My fragile male ego might implode if I have to do it over and over and over…. Yeah, I see you cackling with glee as your eyes light up thinking about it!)

Thank you, fans, for allowing Martha and me the chance to work on stories together and deliver them to you.

Ad Aeternitatem,
Michael Anderle

Waking Magic (1) - Release of Magic (2) - Protection of Magic (3) - Rule of Magic (4) - Dealing in Magic (5) - Theft of Magic (6) - Enemies of Magic (7) - Guardians of Magic (8)

The Soul Stone Mage Series

* Sarah Noffke and Martha Carr *

House of Enchanted (1) - The Dark Forest (2) - Mountain of Truth (3) - Land of Terran (4) - New Egypt (5) - Lancothy (6) - Virgo (7)

The Kacy Chronicles

* A.L. Knorr and Martha Carr *

Descendant (1) - Ascendant (2) - Combatant (3) - Transcendent (4)

The Midwest Magic Chronicles

* Flint Maxwell and Martha Carr*

The Midwest Witch (1) - The Midwest Wanderer (2) - The Midwest Whisperer (3) - The Midwest War (4)

The Fairhaven Chronicles

* with S.M. Boyce *

Glow (1) - Shimmer (2) - Ember (3) - Nightfall (4)